"From now on," he said, "bu_____
back under the covers if you l_____
of the twins in the middle of the night.
I've got it."

"I'll try." She glanced up at him, shaking her head with a smile. "Are you even real?"

"Here," he said, taking her hand and putting it on his cheek. "Real?"

He hadn't meant to do that.

She held his gaze, and parts of him he'd suppressed for months came back to life.

Then suddenly they were kissing and he wasn't even sure who leaned closer to whose lips first. Her hands were on his back, his shoulders and then his hair as they deepened the kiss, and his were inching under her long T-shirt, higher and higher until he felt bare skin. He felt her shudder and he drew her closer.

"Waaah! Waah-waah!"

Noooo.

* * *

_____ WYOMING MULTIPLES:

Dear Reader,

Coming home to Wedlock Creek, Wyoming, isn't easy for former soldier Nick Garroway. His relationships with his father and brother are complicated to say the least. But he made a promise to check up on a single mother of infant twins. A quick stop at Brooke Timber's house to make sure she and her little ones are all right and then he'll be back on the road, buying that faraway ranch he's always dreamed of.

Thing is, Brooke needs help. And so Nick unexpectedly finds himself the temporary live-in caregiver of her baby boys, his heart being tugged in all kinds of new directions...

I hope you enjoy Brooke and Nick's story! I love to hear from readers. Hop on over to my website, melissasenate.com, for more info and write me at MelissaSenate@yahoo.com with comments and questions or just to say hello. Also, feel free to follow me on Twitter, @melissasenate, and find me on Facebook as Melissa Senate, particularly if you don't mind seeing lots of photos of my adorable dog and cat!

Warmest regards,

Melissa Senate

A Promise
for the Twins

Melissa Senate

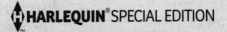
HARLEQUIN® SPECIAL EDITION

Recycling programs
for this product may
not exist in your area.

ISBN-13: 978-1-335-57395-7

A Promise for the Twins

Copyright © 2019 by Melissa Senate

This edition published by arrangement with Harlequin Books S.A.

For questions and comments about the quality of this book,
please contact us at CustomerService@Harlequin.com.

® and TM are trademarks of Harlequin Enterprises Limited or its
corporate affiliates. Trademarks indicated with ® are registered in the
United States Patent and Trademark Office, the Canadian Intellectual
Property Office and in other countries.

Printed in U.S.A.

Melissa Senate has written many novels for Harlequin and other publishers, including her debut, *See Jane Date*, which was made into a TV movie. She also wrote seven books for Harlequin's Special Edition line under the pen name Meg Maxwell. Her novels have been published in over twenty-five countries. Melissa lives on the coast of Maine with her teenage son; their rescue shepherd mix, Flash; and a lap cat named Cleo. For more information, please visit her website, melissasenate.com.

For Max, with love.

Chapter One

Nick Garroway had three items on his to-do list for this warm and breezy July morning, and the sooner he dealt with the complicated first two, the sooner he'd get to the third—the prize.

One: check on a woman named Brooke Timber. Make sure she was all right/see if she needed anything. He had no idea if Brooke was still pregnant or had given birth. He'd soon find out.

Two: visit his father whether the man liked it or not, despite the fact that Nick's brother would probably punch him in the face if he stepped foot in the family home.

Three: buy a ranch far, far away from Wedlock Creek. He envisioned a couple thousand acres, a white farmhouse with a weathered barn, a few dogs from the local humane society running around, a horse, a hundred head of cattle to start, maybe some sheep. Definitely chickens.

Nick parked his Jeep in the public lot by the Wedlock Creek town square and got out, stretching his legs. It had been a long drive from Texas, and he'd started well before the crack of dawn. With his aviator sunglasses on and his brown Stetson pulled down low, he headed toward Main Street. He wondered if Dee's Diner was still around. He hoped so. He could use a big plate of scrambled eggs, bacon, and Dee's really good hash browns with peppers and onions. And lots of coffee. An entire urn wouldn't be enough to deal with the second item on his list.

He glanced up the street, which was bustling already at just before 8:00 a.m. with folks heading to work, into the coffee shop, the bakery, a line of little kids in Wedlock Creek Day Camp T-shirts turning into the gated entrance to the park just a few feet away, and lots of dog walkers.

He was glad to see Dee's Diner still there, at the end of Main Street, with a swanky new sign depicting a cowgirl roping a plate of pancakes atop the door. Small towns were all about mom-and-pop businesses, and Dee's must be doing well. He headed in, taking off the shades and hat and hoping no one would recognize him and make small talk. Nick wasn't in the mood.

And who'd recognize him anyway? He hadn't been back in Wedlock Creek in almost five years, since his brother had let him know he hadn't been welcome that Thanksgiving and should spend the holiday from now on in Afghanistan "since he preferred military life and combat over his family." His father hadn't said otherwise, so Nick had stopped bothering to come home on leave or between tours.

His brother's scowling face came to mind. Good

God. The thought of dealing with Brandon Garroway today almost made him lose his appetite. But Nick was starting a new life, and the only way to actually get going on a new one was to square away the old one. Nick needed to square away things with his dad.

He pulled open the door to Dee's Diner and took in the delicious aromas of pancakes, French toast and bacon. And coffee. His appetite was saved.

Nick was greeted a warm hello, led to a small booth by a waitress with a coffeepot in her hand and, within five minutes, his order was before him, along with today's *Wedlock Creek Gazette*.

The home fries were as good as he remembered. As he ate, he flipped through the newspaper, full of town happenings and local sports, ads and classifieds. He already had three solid leads on ranches a few hours or so from Wedlock Creek, but figured he'd check out any listings the *Gazette* might have. He scanned them—all too close to town. He did want to live in Wyoming—his roots were here—but a few hours' distance between him and the Garroways sounded about right.

Nick forked a bite of eggs and bacon and was about to close the paper when a name in a boxed ad taking half the page caught his eye.

Nanny Wanted

Experienced, caring, tenderhearted nanny sought for relatively easy three-month-old twins. Monday–Friday, 9–1. Hours negotiable. If interested, call/text Brooke Timber: (307) 555-1022

So, she'd had the twins. Nick didn't know anything about Brooke Timber other than that she was very pretty—he'd seen a photo—had long brown hair, enormous pale brown eyes and a dimple in her left cheek, and that someone he owed a big favor to, the ultimate favor, had "done her wrong" and wanted to rectify that. Between having two reasons to come home to Wedlock Creek—making good on a promise to a fallen soldier and dealing with his dad—here he was.

He finished his mug of coffee and was grateful when the waitress appeared with a fresh pot and refilled. He tore out the ad so he'd have Brooke Timber's telephone number. He'd already googled her address and had that memorized. She lived over on Oak Lane, which was within walking distance from here, a couple houses off Main Street.

He stared at the words *relatively easy* in the ad. That had to be a good sign that Brooke was okay, that she was fine and he could cross her off his to-do list after a quick visit to her home. A couple of guys in his unit had been fathers, and one talked a lot about his very colicky baby but had always said he'd give anything to be with the screamer rather than thousands of miles away.

Once upon a time, Nick would have said he didn't know anything about that. Or babies at all. But now the stirring of a memory socked him in the gut, a little face with big dark eyes and shiny black wisps of curls, fifteen pounds at most in his arms, and he closed his eyes against it, downing half the mug of coffee to keep the face at bay.

Take care of business, he told himself. *Check on Brooke Timber, talk to your dad and then you'll be*

*home free to buy a ranch. The land and hard work will
make you forget anything you need to.*

The waitress glanced at him with her coffeepot lifted,
and he nodded and smiled. Oh yeah, bring on the third
cup. He'd need it.

Waiting in a long line at Java Jane's coffee shop,
single-mother Brooke Timber hoped her three-month-
old twins wouldn't get too fidgety and start screeching
before she could order a large iced coffee. She glanced
at the huge sign on the wall, the menu handwritten in
colored chalk. Small, plain iced coffee: $1.95. What she
really wanted was a large iced mocha with whipped
cream, but that was $5.45. And forget the cherry Danish
in the display case. She could bake something at home
for free—if she could find the fifteen minutes to stand
still at her counter with flour and eggs.

Money was tight. Time was tight. Brooke's nerve
endings were tight.

"Ga ba!" Mikey gurgled from his stroller, waving his
little chew toy, which he promptly threw on the floor
with a big smile.

Brooke scooped up the sticky orange toy and shoved
it in her stroller bag. Yes, fine, things weren't easy.
She'd known that would be the case. A single mother
with baby twins, no family, trying to run a business—
Brooke was a wedding planner—with four competitors
in town? Her bank accounts, both personal and business, were dwindling. She could not, it turned out, "do
it all"—at once.

"Ba ba!" Morgan gurgled at his brother and threw
his own chew toy on the ground.

Brooke's heart melted at Morgan's thrilled, gummy grin and snatched up the toy; those happy faces of her boys never failed to ground her. Yes, she was stretched to the limit. But look at what she had. These two little dumplings: heathy, adorable babies. Before they were born, Brooke didn't have a relative left in the world. Now she had two precious children. Life was good. A challenge, but good.

"Didja hear the news?" the barista was saying to the woman in front of her. Brooke was next in line and could not wait to be sipping her iced coffee, back out in the gorgeous sunshine. She planned to take Mikey and Morgan to the park, spread out a blanket, and she and the twins could watch their favorite nature show: two squirrels chasing each other up and down a particular tree with huge green leaves. Then she'd take them home for their nap and develop a plan to bring in more business. Of course, she'd lost out on potential clients, even when she'd had a part-time nanny—single motherhood made things that much harder on a new parent—so she had no idea how she thought she'd bring in new business with *no* childcare. The good news was that her industry—weddings—was *big* business in Wedlock Creek.

Despite being a small Wyoming town, Wedlock Creek was famous for its century-old wedding chapel, which came with a beautiful legend: couples who married there would be blessed with multiples. Some scoffed at the legend but there were multiples—twins, triplets, quadruplets and even two sets of quintuplets—all over town, so there had to be something to the legend, or just something in the water.

Weddings, particularly at the chapel for those who wanted many babies at once, were the name of the game here. There were *five* wedding planners in town, including two newbies who didn't scare Brooke the way the two other established ones did. But none of her competition was trying to keep their beloved late grandmother's twenty-seven-year-old business, Dream Weddings, going. Brooke *was*. And she couldn't let her grandmother down. No husband, no nanny and very busy little twins aside.

"The Satler sisters are engaged!" the barista exclaimed, handing the woman in front of Brooke her change. "Isn't that incredible?"

Brooke's ears perked right up. The Satler triplets had gotten engaged?

When the woman moved to the pick-up area, Brooke rushed herself and the stroller to the counter.

"Did you just say the Satler triplets got engaged last night?" Brooke asked the barista. "All *three* of them?"

"Yup, it's true!" the barista said. "And I hear they want a triple ceremony and a lavish reception."

Brooke's eyes widened, her mind whirling. A triple wedding. She would estimate the guest list at five hundred. Maybe 550.

"Isn't that wonderful?" the barista cooed. "All three engaged on the same night, at the same time, in different locations. The boyfriends planned the whole thing. So sweet and romantic!"

"*So* romantic!" Brooke agreed, turning the stroller around and heading for the door. Forget the iced coffee that she could also make for free at home. She had a triple wedding to secure! She rushed the two blocks back to her house, with her mind hard at work.

"Ba ga ba!" Mikey gurgled as Brooke pushed the stroller up the walkway to her front door.

She paused and bit her lip. The boys would miss the squirrels. They loved watching those furry critters chase each other. "I promise to take you to see Lenny and Squiggy later," she told them, opening the front door and wheeling the stroller through.

The names she'd given the squirrels were a necessary reminder of her grandmother, who used to laugh her head off while binge-watching episodes of her favorite old show, *Laverne & Shirley.* Lenny and Squiggy were two goofballs, just like the squirrels. And for her grandmother's legacy, Brooke would focus right now on Dream Weddings.

She took the twins from their stroller, and with one in each arm, headed into the Dream Weddings office, off the hallway. Her grandmother had turned a first-floor bedroom into an office and installed a door to the outside, with a porch, a hand-painted white wooden sign hanging from ornate iron scrolls, and lush satin white drapery in the bay window that was reminiscent of a gorgeous wedding gown.

With the twins in their baby swings beside the desk, she sat and turned on her laptop and created a Dream Weddings possibilities file for her prospective triplet clients. She talked through her ideas to Mikey and Morgan, two sets of big blue-green-hazel eyes hanging on her every word. Mikey got fussy, but a brisk walk around the office, with a back rub and extra-animated talk of pretty flowers and the best bands in the county, calmed him right down.

Forty minutes later, she finished her proposal, forcing herself to wait until the acceptable-to-call hour of 9:00 a.m., and then she phoned Suzannah Satler, the one triplet she knew from the knitting class she'd taken right before the twins were born. Brooke offered congratulations and her services as owner of Dream Weddings, "a full-service wedding planning company, right here in Wedlock Creek." Because of that knitting class and how open and chatty Suzannah had been, Brooke knew quite a bit about the Satler triplets—that they loved country music, the color hot pink and all things glam. Brooke was able to excite Suzannah over the phone in one carefully crafted sentence.

The Satler sisters were due at Dream Weddings at 10:00 a.m. to discuss. Yes, yes, yes!

"I'm back!" she trilled to Morgan and Mikey, waving her hands in the air like a lunatic. Or just like a very excited wedding planner who *had to* sign the Satler sisters.

She plucked the twins from their swings, put them in their baby seats and carried them upstairs. She changed their diapers, then settled them against her on the glider chair for a made-up story about their favorite squirrels. Their little eyes drooping, Brooke carefully transferred each back into his baby seat, praying they wouldn't wake up.

Yes, success! With an eye on the time, she brought the carriers into her bedroom, set them on the floor and opened her closet door. Thank heavens she'd showered this morning. At 4:50 a.m., she'd taken a fast, hot shower, with the baby monitor on the sink, since the twins woke at five o'clock and, if she wanted to shower in peace, she had to do it very, very early. She looked through her closet, nodding at her elegant white pantsuit. Very Satler sisters. She took off her T-shirt and shorts and put on the pretty outfit, adding a watercolor-patterned silk scarf and three-inch peep-toe red fabric heels, which were also very Satler sisters. A quick application of pressed powder, mascara, and lipstick, ponytail off and hair fluffed, a dab of Chanel No. 19, and voilà—the harried single mother turned into the sign-with-me businesswoman. She stared at herself in the mirror, almost amazed at the transformation.

Carrying a baby seat in each hand, she headed back downstairs, on heels she wasn't used to anymore, and went into her office. She gently placed the baby seats under the big ornate desk; its backing completely obscured them from view of the sofa, where her clients would sit.

Also under the desk was a complete stash of baby paraphernalia: diapers, bottles, pacifiers, chew toys, burp cloths and an extra set of pajamas. A single mother without childcare for the time being had to be at the ready.

Brooke had timed the appointment for the twins' usual midmorning naptime, and if things went her way, she would have forty-five minutes to an hour and a half of blessed silence to conduct business with the Satler sisters. Her former nanny, a wonderful, patient saint of a woman, had had to take four to five weeks off to help her daughter, the new mother of twin babies herself. That was two weeks ago. Brooke had had interview after interview with prospective nannies, but for one reason or another, none was right for the job.

One applicant had reeked of marijuana. Another said she couldn't stand the sound of crying, but "that's what binkies were for, right?" A very loud talker insisted that Morgan and Mikey should be separated in the home to ensure independence from each other starting at the most tender of ages. And then there was the one great prospect, who burst into tears during the interview because she was having fertility issues and ran out the door.

I can do this, Brooke chanted to herself in her head. The lack of childcare had presented problems during the past couple of weeks, but Brooke had managed to bring in one client—a small New Year's Eve wedding, at the stroke of midnight. She'd signed that bride earlier this week, with the twins napping under her desk, and her new client none the wiser. Three other prospective clients had slipped through her fingers because of the lack of childcare, but her babies came first. They always would.

For you guys and for gram, she thought, *I'm going to secure the Satler sisters' business.* A triple wedding, particularly Satler style, would mean being back in the black instead of the scary red she was in now. It would mean saving her grandmother's business. The Kardashian-esque Satlers were very popular in town, and signing them would have new brides beating down her door.

She heard a car pull up into the driveway and three doors slam, then the chatter of voices as the Satler sisters approached the Dream Weddings entrance. Brooke got up to open the door and welcome them. Last thing she needed was for the doorbell to wake the twins.

"Congratulations!" Brooke said, giving each triplet a quick hug.

"We're so excited!" Samantha Satler said as the women sat down on the sofa. "Of course we want the ceremony at the Wedlock Creek Chapel, and Suze said you mentioned the Wellington Hotel's grand ballroom—that is *exactly* where we want to have the reception!"

Ha! She knew it. The tall, slender, blonde Satlers, who each wore a different-colored pastel leather cowboy hat, super-skinny jeans, and high-heeled hot-pink perforated cowboy boots, liked bling. Their engagement rings, matching big square diamonds, twinkled on their fingers.

Brooke launched into her plans, giving each sister a handout bullet-pointing their Dream Weddings possibilities for their triple wedding. From the knitting class, she knew the triplets worshipped Carrie Underwood and never missed an area concert, so she'd listed ten fabulous country bands with Carrie-esque female vocalists. A mix of local small businesses and companies in the nearby big town of Brewer, for everything from flowers—the sisters loved white roses—to catering—all three were gluten free, which was another tidbit she'd learned from Beginning Knitting—and Brooke's most trusted printing shops, for exquisite shades of barely-pink invitations and the most delicate velum.

"It's like you're in our heads!" Samantha Sattler trilled. "This is amazing!"

Suzannah Sattler flipped through the handout. "I agree! Okay, so can we talk about the Wellington Hotel's grand ballroom and what we envision for tables and—"

"WAAH! WAAH-WAAH!"

Oh foo. Brooke bit her lip and felt her cheeks flame. She forced a smile. "Excuse me. Just one moment," she said to the sisters, and then she bent under the desk to give Mikey's seat a gentle rock. "There, there," she whispered to Mikey, who was screeching bloody murder. Morgan, miraculously, was still fast asleep.

"Omigod," Shelley said. "Do you have a *baby* under your desk?"

Brooke's cheeks now burned. She quickly told them about her nanny—or lack thereof—situation. She caught the triplets sliding each other uncomfortable glances.

And then it happened.

The worst possible thing, at the worst possible moment.

The unmistakable smell of…baby poop filled the air.

"Ugh, gross!" Samantha said, pinching her nose closed.

Suzannah's face crinkled in disgust and she waved the air in front of her. "Oh God, I think I'm making it worse."

"We're having lunch with our soon-to-be mothers-in-law in an hour and now we'll smell like baby dung!" Shelley muttered.

Brooke stood and pulled out the baby seat, unlatched Mikey and held him in her arms. He screamed, making little fists. "I'll just change him and we can get right back to discussing your dream wedding," Brooke said, trying to keep the pleading out of her voice. She grabbed a diaper and the pack of wipes from her stash under the desk and hoisted Mikey up. "I'll be right back—"

She was about to flee into the restroom when a man she'd never seen before—tall, dark and crazy hot—opened the door to Dream Weddings and walked inside. He was holding her ad from the *Gazette*. Dear Lord, was he here to apply for the job as her nanny? This guy? He reminded her physically of every actor who'd ever played Superman. Down to the piercing blue eyes.

The Satler triplets, who'd been about to run out, stopped and stared at him. Newly engaged or not, a gorgeous specimen of man was a gorgeous specimen of man.

But then Mikey let out a high-pitched shriek that could shatter a window. Shelley slammed her hands over her ears. A wail came from under the desk. Now Morgan was crying too.

First an explosive poop diaper. Then an applicant—an incredibly sexy one—for the nanny job, walking right into one of the most important meetings of her career. Now two babies screaming bloody murder.

She could kiss the lavish triplet wedding at the Wellington adieu.

The stranger looked at Brooke, then at the baby in her arms and glanced toward the desk, where more wailing could be heard, if not seen. Suddenly, Morgan stopped crying, though she was sure it would be short-lived. He eyed the frowning triplets edging toward the door. "Looks like you have your hands full," he said to Brooke, setting the nanny-wanted ad on the credenza. "Allow me. I'm pretty good with babies."

He stepped toward her, arms extended as if to take her child, and Brooke stepped back, shielding Mikey from him.

"Listen, bucko, I don't know you," she said.

God, he really did have the most gorgeous blue eyes with long dark lashes. The slightest of five-o'clock shadows graced his strong jawline.

Shelley Satler was staring at him. "Hey, aren't you Nick Garroway?" she asked him. "You were a year ahead of us in high school. You played football and baseball, if I remember correctly."

"You do," he said with a smile. "And of course I remember you three. The lovely and smart Satler triplets. Copresidents of your class. One of you—maybe *all* of you, at various points—used to babysit my younger brother. It's very nice to see you again."

The triplets beamed and swooned and chatted with this Nick Garroway about old times.

So, he wasn't an axe murderer. Or baby-napper. The Satlers were four years older than Brooke, so Nick was out of high school by the time Brooke would have been a freshman. She would have had a serious crush on him if she'd known him back then.

He stepped closer again. "May I?" he said, reaching for Mikey. "If you direct me to a changing area, I'll take care of this ASAP and you can continue your meeting."

Uh, I guess? How weird was this? She handed him the diaper, the wipes, and her precious baby son, and pointed toward the restroom, where she had a changing station set up. "Where I can see your every move," she whispered to him, and he nodded as he took Mikey inside, keeping the door half open. The Satlers couldn't see into the bathroom from where they stood—thank heavens—but they could all hear him humming a lullaby. Brahms's.

"Well, Brooke, looks like you found your new nanny," Shelley said with a grin. "And just in time."

"You mean her new *manny*," Samantha corrected,

with a wiggle of her eyebrows. "Male plus nanny equals manny."

"A *hot* manny," Suzannah put in. She grinned at Brooke, tipping her lemon-yellow leather cowboy hat at her. "Brooke, you seriously impress! Listen, why don't you write up a comprehensive plan for our wedding, with all the new info we discussed here today, and we'll go over it, but we're 99 percent going to hire you and Dream Weddings for our big day."

Thank you, universe.

And thank you, Hot Manny.

The man himself emerged from the restroom, with Mikey smiling and grabbing Nick's chiseled jawline. "Now this little dude smells like snips and snails and puppy dog tails and everything else good that little boys are made of."

Brooke stared at him, speechless. Where on earth had he come from? Was he even *from* earth?

Each Satler sister winked at Brooke, made a little fuss over Mikey, said goodbye to Nick with one last admiring glance at him and then left.

"The job is yours," Brooke said to him as she pointed at the ad. "Can you start immediately? I guess you already have."

The Hot Manny tilted his head and stared at her. "Oh, I'm not here about the job."

Chapter Two

"I'm confused," Brooke said, reaching for the baby in Nick's arms.

He almost didn't want to let the little guy go. He liked how the sturdy small weight felt in his arms, against his chest. He'd been surprised by that back in Afghanistan—how satisfying, how gratifying it was to hold a tiny baby. How hard it was to hand the baby over.

Some things just sneaked up on a former US Army combat soldier unexpectedly. Like how raw he felt about his reason for being here. The sooner he gave back Mikey, the sooner he'd have to explain why he'd come. He had no idea how that conversation was going to go.

"You're *not* here to apply for the nanny position?" she asked, taking the baby and giving Mikey a kiss on his cheek. Mikey gurgled and then immediately spit up on the jacket of Brooke's white pantsuit. It had to take courage to wear something like that with baby twins.

She barely seemed to notice. She reached under the desk, grabbed a burp cloth, dabbed the drool, tossed the cloth on her shoulder, and then put Mikey in his swing and transferred the twin beside him. With both babies occupied and playing with chew toys attached to the swing, she turned her attention back to him.

Those driftwood-brown eyes of hers had stopped him in his tracks when he'd seen that one photo of her on Will Parker's phone. Intelligent and assessing. And tired now. He could see the dark shadows and the pull of exhaustion. He'd known she was pretty. But the instant wham of connection he'd felt when he'd first laid eyes on her in person was anything but expected.

"No," he said. "I was on my way to see you and happened to notice the ad for a nanny in the *Gazette*. I ripped it out so I'd have your phone number if you weren't at home."

But she had been at home. Fortified with caffeine from the diner, he'd pulled up in front of her house, taking note of the well-kept small white Cape Cod with black shutters and a red door, the lawn tended to, two black-and-white cats snoozing on a padded swing, two cars in the driveway—one a brand-new Range Rover that must have cost a mint. He now realized the Range Rover probably belonged to the Satlers. The second car was a decade-old Honda. He'd breathed a sigh of relief that Brooke Timber was clearly doing fine and that he could be on his way to dealing with number two on his list. But then he'd heard the sound of babies wailing and high-pitched shrieks from adults, and that hadn't sounded too okay, so he'd followed the noise to the side door, a business entrance, and marched in.

Brooke hadn't looked fine at all, not in the slightest. He'd sprung into action, as was his wont, and somehow the four women in the room had managed to mistake him for a nanny.

At six foot two, 185 pounds, with a small tattoo of "purple mountain majesties" on his left bicep and size-thirteen black work boots, he wouldn't have thought anyone would confuse him with an applicant for a baby-sitting job—*Gazette* ad in hand or not.

"Ah! So you must be a prospective client," Brooke said. "When's the big day?"

Client? Big day? What was she talking about? Then he remembered the Satler triplets with their huge rock engagement rings and the shingle outside her side door. Brooke was a wedding planner.

"Good God, no," he said with a shake of his head. Now he was taken for a groom? "I'm not the marrying kind."

She raised an eyebrow. "Everyone is the marrying kind. My clients have been all sorts. Last year, a search-and-rescue worker fell in love with a man who lived off the grid, in the mountains, without electricity or running water. She got him to upgrade to a real cabin with the basics and even Wi-Fi, but they're way out in the woods, eating only what they forage themselves."

He smiled. "I'm surprised that a woman who'd live in a cabin in the woods with a mountain man would even hire a wedding planner."

"I know, but the groom scoffed at everything she suggested, and only when his bride threatened to run back to civilization did he agree to let her handle the wedding her way, with him *in mind*. Her job was so demanding that she had no time or interest in figuring it all out, so she hired me. I planned a small, quiet ceremony on the bank of the Wedlock Creek river, with the mountain as a backdrop. The 'caterer' was a fisherman, who made an amazing clambake. The 'band' was a fiddler. But guess who put on a rented tuxedo to make his bride happy? Yup."

"Well, I'll be," he said on a laugh. "I guess you never know. That may be the only thing I do know for sure."

She laughed too, and for a moment he couldn't take his eyes off her. She had silky, straight brown hair past her shoulders, a dimple in her left cheek and, though he was usually drawn to more casual women, he liked the fancy outfit and little scarf at her neck and the pointy, polished high heels. Maybe because she gave the appearance of having it all together. And whether or not she did was the reason he was here.

"So, what *can* I do for you, Nick Garroway?"

Brooke looked happy and peaceful at the moment, and he didn't want to spoil it. But she was staring at him with those big brown eyes. Waiting for an explanation.

"I'm newly medically retired from the army," he said. "For the past month, I've been recuperating from a foot injury at a base in Texas, after eleven years as a combat soldier in Afghanistan."

"Thank you for your service," she said, her voice turning hesitant and her entire body stiffening. "And you came to see me because…"

He could tell she was bracing herself. "Will Parker was in my unit."

She glanced at the babies in their swings, her shoulders slumping. Then she lifted her chin and let out a breath.

Her cell phone rang in the silence of the room.

"I'll let voice mail get it," she said, then dropped down in her desk chair as if her legs had been about to give out on her.

The phone stopped ringing, but before he could say a word, the annoying ringtone started up again. He could tell she needed a breather—but from *him* and what else he had to say. "Take the call, Brooke. I'll keep an eye on the twins."

"Really?" she asked. "Even though you're not here about the job?"

He nodded. "Go ahead. Might as well while I'm here."

She snatched the phone as if it were a lifeline. "Brooke Timber of Dream Weddings speaking. How may I help you?"

He kneeled down in front of the baby swings to make funny faces at the twins, but he was distracted by Brooke—how hard she was listening, how tired she looked, how rigid her shoulders were now, probably from his news about being here because he knew Will.

The twins' father.

"Absolutely, Francesca," she said into the phone. "The salmon is out, the sole almondine is in. I'll make it happen."

Brooke put down the phone. "One of my clients wants to switch her menu. Someone told her that salmon was dated and that she should go with the hipper sole."

He smiled, but a call like that would push him off the edge. Salmon was dated? Sole was hip? *What?* "Bride's wish is your command?"

"Pretty much. Unless they're dead wrong and I need to do reality checks. But if sole almondine will make Francesca Perry happy? Done."

"You're like a wedding genie," he said.

She gave him a bittersweet smile. "Well, my grandmother named this business Dream Weddings when she opened up shop in this very room, twenty-seven years ago. I promised her in the hospice last year that I'd run the business just as she had, with everything she taught me. My job is to make brides' dreams come true for their big day. And no dream is silly or wrong or too small or too big. That's what Gram always said."

A wistful expression filled her eyes, and he could see how much she missed her grandmother. He knew from Will Parker that Brooke was all alone in the world— no parents, no other family. Couldn't be easy raising twins under those circumstances. *And* running a business, to boot.

Family businesses, family ties. He also full well knew the grip those could have. He'd let go. But not everyone could or would, was willing, or wanted to. Brooke spoke of her grandmother with love and reverence and seemed to truly like her job, so it was clear her family ties weren't like the rope he'd had to cut with a sharp knife.

"Well," she said. "Why don't we talk in the house. It's close to lunchtime for Morgan and Mikey."

He looked at Brooke in her fancy outfit, with two babies to feed, no nanny and work to do, given the project she had in front of her to secure the Satlers' weddings. And then he heard Will Parker's voice in his head, usually so light and full of devilish mischief, asking something of Nick with regret and sorrow in his tone.

He could certainly be of help while he was here, relaying Will's message.

"May I?" he asked, ready to scoop up Morgan. The little guy wore orange-and-white-striped footsie pajamas. He—and Mikey—both looked a lot like Brooke, but he could see hints of Will.

"Sure, thanks," she said, picking up Mikey.

The beautiful baby boy in his arms reached up and poked his cheek. He smiled. "Hi. I'm Nick."

Morgan drooled in response.

Brooke laughed and pulled a burp cloth off her shoulder. "Here. I made the rookie mistake of not having this close enough earlier."

He took the burp cloth and gave the little lips a dab, then put the cloth on his shoulder, but that felt remarkably stupid, so he just held on to it.

He followed her through an arched doorway, into a living room with a baby play area off to the side. A big carton with one side open was against the wall, with a picture of a white bookcase on the front, a set of instructions and a toolbox next to it.

"Haven't gotten around to putting it together yet?" he asked.

She sighed. "I keep meaning to. It's for the twins' nursery. But then it's time to feed them or put them down for their nap, or the phone rings or a client comes over. This morning I got the twins out for the gorgeous summer morning air and a Java Jane's run, fully intending to come home and at least start the bookcase, but then the Satler sisters got engaged and securing them as clients became everything."

He nodded. "Well, sounds like you did just that."

"Thanks to you. If you hadn't walked through the door and reminded them of high school before changing Mikey while singing a lullaby, they would have run screaming out of my office, straight to my competition."

"Well, then I've already fulfilled some of my promise," he said.

She tilted her head. "Promise? What do you mean?" The moment the words were out, she slightly shook her head as if she didn't really want to know and kept her gaze off him, so he stayed quiet.

She put Mikey in the baby seat on the kitchen table, and he did the same with Morgan beside him. She made up two bottles, and he couldn't help but notice the sink was full of dishes, despite the dishwasher right next to it. A basket of laundry—whether clean or dirty, he wasn't sure—was beside one of the chairs. Clearly Brooke needed help—the nanny she'd advertised for so that she could operate her business and take care of the everyday stuff.

Yup, she wasn't waiting for his answer, which made him think she wasn't ready to hear what he had to say. She went into the living room and put the two bottles on the coffee table, then came back into the kitchen and picked up Morgan. He picked up Mikey and followed her, settling next to her on the couch.

He watched the way she laid Morgan slightly upright, giving the baby the bottle. He did the same with Mikey, then was about to answer her question. About the promise.

"Have multiples yourself?" she asked before he could. "Is that why you're so good with Morgan and Mikey?"

He almost laughed. "Kids? *Me?* No. Not the marrying kind, not the dad kind. I got some unexpected baby-care experience overseas. Long story." And one he wasn't interested in talking about. The less he thought about what he'd been through in Afghanistan, the better.

"Well, it's nice to have someone else to help so they can both eat at the same time," she said. "I had a wonderful nanny the first two months, but she had to leave town to help her own daughter. I guess I've been so focused on taking care of the twins that I've neglected everything else. I'm sure you noticed the state of the kitchen."

"You're busy and on your own," he said. "A single mother, raising baby twins alone, running a business— something has to be put off, and it sure as hell should be the dishes."

She laughed. "Right? I agree." The smile faded fast and she slid a glance his way.

He tilted the bottle up as Mikey drank it down, then inwardly sighed. This was not going to be easy.

"So, about the promise you made," she said. She closed her eyes for a second as if bracing herself again, then opened them, keeping her attention on the baby in her arms.

He cleared his throat. "Will asked me to check on you and to pass along a message."

She stared at him hard. "He asked you to check on me? Why? It's been nearly a year since he sent me a Dear Jane email, so I'm surprised he cares one iota about me—or the twins."

"Will was killed six weeks ago," he said as gently as he could. But there was no gentle way to say such a thing.

He lowered his head out of respect for the fallen soldier, and to give Brooke some privacy with her emotions.

"I didn't know," she whispered. "What happened?"

"IED—improvised explosive device. I might have been killed if he hadn't thrown himself on top of me. He took the brunt of it."

"Oh God." She shook her head.

"Will and I had never been close or even friends, really. But we were from the same hometown, and that connected us. Maybe that was why he saved my life. Or maybe he'd always had that in him and I didn't know it."

"That he could be a hero?" she asked, tears in her eyes.

He nodded. "Will liked to make jokes, pull pranks. Never all that serious about anything. And then he saved my life. Can't get more serious than throwing yourself on another soldier to protect him."

They were quiet for a moment, and she nodded.

"Will was fading," he finally continued, "but I could see he wanted to tell me something. He said there was a woman from Wedlock Creek, a beautiful, kind, good person named Brooke Timber, who he did wrong. Ghosted her when she told him she was pregnant with twins, then sent an email that he wasn't cut out for fatherhood and they'd all be better off without him."

Her lips tightened. "That's almost verbatim. All two lines of the email."

He glanced at her for a moment. She was waiting for him to continue. "Then Will said, 'Garroway, will you check on her when you get home? Make sure she's all right? See if she needs anything?' And I assured him I would. The last thing he said was, 'Tell her I'm sorry.

She deserved better.'" He winced, remembering the look on Parker's face. The regret.

She smoothed her hand over Morgan's wispy dark hair. "Your daddy was a hero," she whispered to the baby. "And he sent a guardian angel to check on us. That's not nothing."

The backs of his eyes stung, and he blinked hard.

"Well, message delivered," she said, slashing a hand under each eye and standing up. "As you can see, we're okay. Everything is okay."

"Waaah!" Morgan started crying, the little face crumpling and turning red.

She closed her eyes and took a breath, then opened them. "I need to burp and change Morgan. Thank you for coming, Nick. You can put Mikey in his swing in the kitchen and let yourself out," she added before rushing from the room with Morgan.

Was she crying? Just emotional? Needing to be alone and get control of herself?

You can let yourself out... He could, indeed. Mission accomplished, right?

But there was no way he was leaving. Because Brooke wasn't all right. And he'd promised the soldier who'd saved his life that he'd make sure she was.

He looked down at the baby in his arms, the blue-green-hazel eyes staring up at him so trustingly.

Nick didn't always get it right, but he wasn't about to get this wrong.

Chapter Three

Brooke got a hold of herself in the bathroom, cuddling Morgan against her. After her five-night stand with Will Parker last year, she'd vowed never to be stupid about a man again. And for a minute there, all she'd wanted was to fling herself into Nick's arms and let him hold her. He was so tall and muscular and kind, and connected to her past and present in a way that had stolen her breath. What she would give for a long hug where she could let someone else be the strong one for just a minute.

No, no, no, she cautioned herself now, staring at her reflection in the mirror as she held her son. Been there, done that—and wouldn't be so dumb again. Last year, grieving for her grandmother and overwhelmed by running Dream Weddings on her own, she'd given into a tall, sexy blond soldier, whose easy smile, soulful eyes and outstretched hand let her believe all kind of foolish things.

Will had been in between tours and had a week to himself in his hometown. They'd met while she'd been walking Paco, a Great Dane she'd been dogsitting, on Main Street. Will, sauntering down the sidewalk, had fussed over the majestic dog, and just like that, she'd had a date the next afternoon. He'd invited her to the rodeo, and after three dates in three days, they were in bed the rest of the week. They'd connected over both losing their parents, over loving Mexican food and margaritas, over their love of the rugged Wyoming countryside and fresh, open air. He'd listened to her talk about growing Dream Weddings and had said, looking seriously and meaningfully into her eyes, that maybe someday soon she'd have a dream wedding of her own.

They'd had the most amazing five days and nights together, and then he'd had to return overseas. There were a few emails that first month, and then he barely responded to hers. When she'd discovered she was pregnant nine weeks after their time together, she'd emailed him the news, having no idea how he'd react. But she hadn't expected him to act like she—and their twins— didn't exist. He'd washed his hands of her, and that was that.

She'd known immediately that Will Parker was about fun and games, but those real moments they'd shared, the connection, had tricked her into letting her guard down. She'd never felt so alone after losing her grandmother, and Will had made her feel part of something, a duo. She'd had no idea how badly she wanted to belong to someone, and for someone to belong to her. But the idea of ever falling for another man had gone right out the window.

Morgan and Mikey were her family. Will had given her the twins. For that she was grateful.

And he'd saved Nick Garroway's life. She would tell her children that their father had died a hero. For that she was also grateful.

And now her precious baby boy was downstairs with someone who was practically a stranger! Where the hell was her judgment? She rushed out of the bathroom, telling herself to breathe.

He's not a stranger, she reminded herself. *The Satlers know him. He came here to fulfill a promise to your babies' father. He can change a diaper and sing a lullaby at the same time. Mikey is fine.*

Was *she* fine, though? She'd been barely able to drag her eyes off Nick Garroway every time they were in the same room together.

She went into the kitchen and stopped in her tracks. Mikey was happy in his baby seat on the table, playing with his chewy attachments. Beside him, on the chair, was the clean laundry she'd neglected for three days, folded and stacked. And Nick Garroway was loading the dishwasher and telling Mikey a story about a lost raccoon named Rocky.

"Everyone was looking for Rocky," Nick was saying. "But no one could find him, Mikey. Guess where he was?" He waited a beat, looking over at the baby. "Yup, you got it. Fast asleep under a pile of leaves!"

She smiled and put Morgan in the seat next to Mikey. "He loads dishwashers. He tells stories. He folds laundry. He changes diapers. He makes good on promises."

He's too good-looking and too helpful. Do not lean into him. He came here for a reason and now he'll be leaving.

Good thing too. Brooke hadn't thought she'd be attracted—even on a purely physical level—to another man for a long time, after the way Will had treated her. And here she was, clearly still very red-blooded. Add in all of Nick's other attributes, and that made him truly dangerous.

He turned and flashed her a smile. "You okay?"

Brooke nodded. "Just needed a minute. You didn't have to do all this," she said. "I'm sure I'll find a nanny soon. I have a lead on a trustworthy possibility, but she's in college and I'd have to work around her hours."

He put a glass in the dishwasher and turned to her. "I've been doing some thinking while I've been rinsing bowls and stacking plates. Remember when I said I wasn't here about the job?"

She nodded, wondering where he was headed with this.

"I might not have come for the job," he said. "But I'm taking it."

She stared at him. He looked dead serious. *"What?"*

"What what? You heard the Satlers. I'm the hot manny."

She laughed. She couldn't help it. She honestly didn't think she'd be able to laugh for at least a few months after the conversation she and Nick had had in the living room fifteen minutes ago.

He *was* hot. Insanely so. She watched him scrape a plate clean and rinse it before putting it in the dishwasher. She looked at the folded baby clothes. She looked at Mikey, so happy in the swing, which meant he'd been burped just right. A half hour ago, she'd been ready to promise him the moon if he'd take the job. But that was before she knew why he'd even sought her out. And why he wanted the job. Heavy stuff. And she'd had enough heavy to last her a few years.

Her phone rang again.

"Could be another bride, Brooke. And with your manny on the job, you might as well as be working."

"We'll finish this conversation in two seconds," she said.

She grabbed her phone. A new client! Yes! The woman envisioned a small and intimate ceremony for family and close friends, at a local wellness retreat a friend owned. Very fast turn-around in a couple of weeks, but only thirty to forty people, tops. *Possible*, Brooke thought, her mind whirling. They made arrangements to meet tomorrow, at 6:00 p.m., for dinner at the woman's fiancé's house. If the Satler triplets were a definite, adding this client for July would mean she could take off the first couple of weeks of August, which were always slow for Dream Weddings, and just be with her twins.

Which would mean needing Nick Garroway as her nanny—manny—until her regular nanny returned. Leanna could take some time off herself and start mid-August. Win-win for everyone.

A temporary manny. A necessary temporary manny.

"Well, I've consulted with myself," Brooke said as she put the phone on the table. "The job is yours. I'll only need help until August first. Then I'll take some time off, and Leanna, my regular nanny, will be ready to come back to work for me."

He nodded. "Sounds good. Oh—and I know your ad

called for hours of nine to one during the week, but I'll make you a deal. I'll be your around-the-clock nanny, as needed—for room and board."

She swallowed. "You mean live here?"

"Temporarily. I'd rather not stay with my family. And I never liked hotels much. Besides, this way, you can work when you need to, not be boxed into someone else's hours."

Even a part-time nanny was very expensive—more than she could afford—but Brooke had always been grateful that necessity would make her limit her work so that she could spend real time with her babies. Now she'd have as-needed care for the twins without spending a penny.

Once again she wondered where Nick Garroway had come from. He was like a miracle—and everything Brooke needed right now.

"I think I'm getting the better deal," she said. "But my grandmother always said not to look a gift horse in the mouth." Especially when that gift horse was clearly a workhorse.

"Good. You get what you need and I make good on that promise. Works for both of us."

She glanced at him. He might be gorgeous and sexy, and too capable with a diaper and a stack of dirty dishes, but he *wasn't* her fantasy in the flesh; he was here because he'd promised her babies' father he'd make sure she and the twins were all right. Will had saved his life; now Nick was doing what he could to save hers. She had to stop thinking of him as a man— somehow, despite how attracted she was to him on a few different levels. He was her nanny, her manny.

But what was sexier than a man saying, "Take a break, I'll handle it. Take that call, I've got the kids. Go rest, I'll load the dishwasher and fold the laundry"?

Nothing was sexier. Which meant Brooke would have to be on guard 24/7.

Because her brain had caught up with her: the hot manny was moving into her house.

Every now and then over the past two hours, Nick would find himself doing something *so* strange, such as dividing a can of Seafood Surprise cat food between the two black-and-white cats rubbing against his leg, and he'd glance up and wonder where the hell he was and what had happened to his life. One minute he was going through his to-do list, checking on Brooke Timber. The next he was a live-in manny—at his own insistence. Caring for very small humans and cats, and making sure one particular woman was A-OK.

What?

He spooned out an equal portion for each cat in their mouse-decorated porcelain bowls, and they attacked it with gusto. After making sure their water bowl was full enough, he washed his hands—cat food kind of stank—and dried them with a little towel with dancing teacups on it. Again: *Where am I? Who am I?*

He found himself a bit surprised at how much he'd actually enjoyed all the stuff he'd taken care of around the house, such as folding the laundry—the tiny pajamas and burp cloths and soft sheets decorated with little dinosaurs. Fixing the storm door that had annoyingly squeaked. Tidying the nursery by putting away storybooks left on the table beside the glider and cleaning up sprinkles of cornstarch on the changing pad. He even liked when those two black-and-white cats jumped on the couch, beside him, and sniffed him, then sat down next to him, grooming their faces.

Nick had been one thing his entire adult life: a soldier. But this? Changing babies' diapers and telling them stories and giving them bottles and rubbing their backs when they cried? Feeding cats? This was something else entirely, and his work in this house was strangely satisfying. He had no clue why this would be the case. Playing house wasn't his thing and he had no interest in making a future of it. So, why did he feel so comfortable here when he should feel the polar opposite?

Maybe it had something to do with how coming home to Wedlock Creek had made him uneasy, unsure how the transition to civilian life would go. He'd been unsettled about the idea of seeing his father and his brother, and once again of having to leave town to start a new life elsewhere. But here in the Timber household, as this manny, of all things, he was in strange, uncharted territory, but with a defined mission for a set amount of time. The new job kept him completely distracted from those other thoughts. Being here was like a balm.

His life at the moment was as if an alien from another planet had plunked him in the least likely existence and said, "This will be weird, but you belong here right now."

That was how he felt. Like he belonged here. But still—and wasn't there always a *but* or a *still*? Something was throwing him. Brooke herself. She drew him in ways he wasn't even clear on. A sexual pull, yes, but it was more than that. When she talked, he understood her, understood the context, understood what she wasn't saying, read her expressions and knew what to say.

When had that ever happened—let alone so instantly? Never. Nick had had rare opportunities for relationships, but he'd always felt the women he dated had spoken a language he didn't understand. It was different with Brooke. And he barely knew her. He didn't know her at all, actually. He'd have to be careful not to get overly involved emotionally.

Just remember you're here on a final mission and you'll be fine, he assured himself. In fact that *was* probably why he felt so comfortable here in the first place. This was a mission, and he knew how to handle those. But all missions came to an end and then a soldier moved on. As a civilian, it would be his job to move on to what came next. His ranch. Waiting for him in sun-drenched, lazy August.

And now, officially the Timber manny for two hours, Nick was on a roll. Brooke had worked on the Satler triplets' file, then taken the nap he'd insisted on, a long, hot shower, eaten the grilled cheese and bacon he'd made for her, and sighed with happy relief when she realized he'd dabbed sunscreen on Morgan and Mikey's faces, arms, and legs, packed their stroller bag and settled them inside the double stroller. Brooke had mentioned something about taking the twins to the park to see their favorite squirrels in an oak tree.

Now she stood by the front door, one hand on the stroller, the other reaching into the tote bag and pulling out her keys. "Oh, I guess I don't need to lock up. You'll do that. Or…" she said, but trailed off.

Or did you want to join us? He had no idea why he could read her so well. She seemed to be both anxious to get the hell away from him and wondering if she should invite him on the outing.

Getting away from him seemed to be winning. He could see it in her eyes, in the way she held herself, which was the opposite of relaxed.

"Here's an idea," he said, wanting to give her the easy out. "I need to go to see my dad, let him know I'm back in town. Then how about we meet here in a couple of hours, and we can sit down and discuss your needs."

"My needs?" she repeated.

"While I'm here, I want to make your life easier. Caring for the twins, helping around the house. Whatever you need, Brooke."

She tilted her head just slightly. "You really want to make good on that promise, don't you." Not a question.

"Of course I do. Will saved my life. I owe him everything."

She took in a breath and nodded. "Well, I guess we're ready to go. Oh, you'll be needing this," she said, pulling a key off the horseshoe keychain and handing it to him. "Front door."

The key felt strange in his palm.

She gave him an awkward smile and then hurried the stroller out the door. Man, it felt weird watching her wheel the twins out of her own house while he waved goodbye on the porch as if he lived here. Which he supposed he did, for the time being. He hooked the keychain onto his own keychain and put it back in his pocket, his gaze on Brooke pushing the stroller up Oak Lane. She turned her head back to him, he held up a hand, and she waved, then crossed the street and disappeared down Main.

Part of him wanted to go after her. Which was nuts. She was a grown woman and had been caring for the twins for the past three months. She could surely handle a trip to watch squirrels on a tree without him hovering. He recognized what he was feeling: responsibility. Well, that and a soft spot for Brooke and those very cute little people.

That made sense to him. It was why he was here, after all.

For a minute he was so overtaken by all these crazy new notions, that he just stood there. But when he noticed a woman two houses down, across the street, staring at him on her porch, he went inside. He'd forgotten what a small town Wedlock Creek was. Neighbors were friendly—but nosy.

"Well, Snowball," he said to the cat with the white smudge on her nose as she rubbed against his leg. "Wish me luck. I'm off to see my dad. Think he's speaking to me?"

Snowball didn't respond, but her sister, Smudge, who had a gray smudge on her black face, stared up at him with her big green eyes.

"Yeah, we'll see," he said, giving each cat a scratch on the back.

He headed for the door and pulled out his keychain, marveling at Brooke's key, which was right next to the gold key to the house he'd grown up in, the one he wasn't welcome in anymore. Once, he'd almost taken it off and chucked it, but he'd been unable to do that. He shook his head and grabbed the fob for his Jeep, trying to forget the other two keys entirely for the moment.

After almost five years, Nick expected the Garroway house to look different, and it did, but he couldn't put his finger on why. Same white Colonial with green shutters and a black door, stone path from the driveway to the three granite steps. But something was different. There were two cars in the driveway, neither of which he recognized. His dad had company? Maybe his brother was over.

And maybe Nick should come back another time.

Or maybe the company part was good. Jeb Garroway had his Kentucky bourbon every night, at 5:45 p.m., and Nick had timed his arrival for 6:05 p.m. and a slightly less uptight version of his father. If he had people over, his dad would be civil.

He glanced at the cars, wondering if one was his brother Brandon's. He hoped not. Nick wished the two of them could fix what was broken between them, but despite being just four years apart in age, the two were never able to get past shouting at each other in person and telling the other to screw off in emails.

Nick rang the bell, then shoved his hands in his pockets. He waited, hearing the footsteps. He probably should have called first, so his father could brace himself, prepare himself. Now he'd open the door and find the black sheep of the family standing there.

The door opened. Jeb Garroway looked as surprised as Nick expected—and he looked good too. Healthier, somehow. His father was tall like Nick, but except for the height and same blue eyes, Nick, like his brother, looked more like their late mother.

"I'm medically retired from the army. Foot injury," Nick blurted out instead of saying hello like a regular son might, a son who felt welcome. "I'm planning to buy a ranch somewhere in the state. Just wanted you to know I was back and what my plans were."

"Foot okay?" his dad asked, looking his son over. Jeb was guarded—Nick could see that—but there was concern in the man's eyes, in his expression. Huh. That was unexpected—and a good sign that maybe the two of them could finally work toward putting their disagreements to rest. The rift between them always felt like a boot pressing on Nick's chest, no matter how he tried not to think of home, of family.

"Almost good as new. I was at a rehab in Texas for the past month. They fixed me up."

His dad nodded. "Well, it's good to see you."

Another good sign. A shock, really.

"You too, Dad." And it was. No matter their differences, Jeb Garroway was his father and he'd always love him, always respect him.

"Why don't you come in, Nick? Have a drink?"

"Sure," he said, surprised this was going so well. He hadn't seen his dad in so long, and the last communication, via email, had been terse. He might not have been welcome at the family house, but he'd always shot off holiday and birthday greetings in emails to his dad, despite being sure they were deleted immediately.

Nick's crime? Twelve years ago, he hadn't gone into the family business. Paper. Garroway Paper. Copy paper, stationery, construction paper, card stock. When

Nick and his brother were young, his father would take them out for hikes through the woods and tell them which trees made which types of paper. Jeb had been making it all up, that the big bur oaks were where the poster board they used for school projects came from. That their report cards were from lodgepole pines. The scrap paper they jotted down grocery lists and reminders on: spruce. Back then Nick had thought the world of paper, and Garroway Paper in particular, was everything. But as he'd gotten older, become a teenager, and developed his own interests and goals, paper had become…paper, something he didn't think much about. Like most people. His father—and brother—to whom paper could be discussed every night over dinner and was, thought Nick was disrespectful. And when he chose the military instead of a business degree and working at Garroway Paper, they both hit the roof.

Even at fourteen years old, his brother, Brandon, had been a mini Jeb Garroway, shaking his finger at Nick for turning his back on family.

Nick could have handled that. But his "betrayal of the family" turned in a direction he didn't see coming, and there was no way to argue, no words to even form. The lump in his chest had blocked all of that.

His brother had blamed him for their mother—frail from cancer treatment—taking a turn for the worse not long after he announced he'd enlisted. Neither had spoken to him at the funeral, which had been between boot camp ending and his deployment.

"You broke her heart!" his brother, who was then just a scrawny teenager, had screamed at him. "Turned your back on the family and tradition! Shame on you."

His father had just hung his head in sorrow and said nothing.

How do you defend yourself against a brokenhearted fourteen-year-old whom you love? You don't. In emails and letters to your brother, you try to explain why you enlisted, but you get back one-line replies, all the same: "go to hell!"

For those first few years, Nick hadn't always been able to come home for holidays, but when it had been possible, he'd showed up, despite the harrowing silences, the seething anger on his brother's face until Brandon had exploded and said that Nick wasn't welcome anymore.

Now here he was, about to walk inside for the first time since then.

He followed his dad and immediately noticed a difference in the place. He'd only been here three or four times over the past twelve years, but he'd always felt the chill, the starkness, the lack of life. His father had loved his mother deeply and mourned her loss, and the curtains had always been drawn, the rooms dark, the flower arrangements his mother had liked in every room no more. Now the house was infused with light. He couldn't put his finger on what else was different, but the living room was...warmer. A huge flowering plant was by the sliding doors to the patio. A bouquet of white roses graced the mantel.

And his dad did look kind of happy instead of his usual serious glumness. And definitely healthier too. Jeb had developed a belly after his wife had passed, but now was fit, with his back straight like a soldier's. That was certainly new. Jeb Garroway had always been something of a hunched-over type, hunched over the books, spreadsheets, his desktop. Suddenly his dad looked athletic. And his thick salt-and-pepper hair was freshly cut instead of its usual bushy, overgrown mop.

Nick had a feeling his dad had a lady in his life. Only thing that would explain such a transformation.

He watched Jeb pour them each two fingers of his favorite bourbon, and Nick thanked him as he handed him a glass.

"A toast," his father said, holding up his glass.

"To?" Nick asked.

"Two things. The first—you're back home, where you belong, so we have a chance for a new start."

Nick almost choked. Who was this man and what had he done with Jeb Garroway? Back where he belonged? New start? A warmth spread inside him as if he'd already swigged his bourbon.

Though…he wasn't quite sure what his dad meant about *belonged*, if Jeb thought Nick would be finally going into the paper business or not. But a new start? He'd take that.

"A new start sounds good, Dad," Nick said, holding up his own glass.

"And the second thing. I'm getting married."

Nick grinned, both at being right about his dad having romance in his life and the big news. "Dad, that's great. Who is she?"

Jeb's blue eyes lit up. "A wonderful woman named Cathy Wylie. She's exactly my age, beautiful, and she cares about paper."

Nick smiled. "She does, huh. Is she in the business?"

"No. She's a yoga instructor. She's teaching me to

elongate my muscles and to breathe." Jeb Garroway took in a deep breath, then let it out in a slow whoosh, complete with arm movements. "We met in line at Java Jane's. She heard me order my usual three shots of espresso with four sugars, and lectured me for a solid minute about the glycemic index. I was like, the *gly-what-ic what-now*? But she was so beautiful, I stood there and listened."

Nick laughed and took a sip of his drink. His father was standing here, talking to Nick, sharing his life, his happiness, his world. Nick hadn't been a part of his dad's universe for so long. Too long. Now things would be different.

"She had me try some crazy green-tea thing," his dad continued. "I didn't like it one bit—in fact I thought it was awful, but I didn't tell her that. Prettiest green eyes you've ever seen. And nothing flusters her. She calls it being grounded and level with the four elements. According to Cathy, paper is rooted in one of the four elements—earth—and a vital part of human communication."

This Cathy Wylie sounded heaven-sent. The woman cared about and respected paper! "I'm very happy for you, Dad. I hope I get to meet her."

"Well, of course you will," Jeb said. "We're having dinner here tomorrow night. Your brother will be joining us. I'd like you to be there."

Nick wasn't so sure *Brandon* would like Nick to be there. He didn't respond, but he had a feeling his expression and the slight nod let his dad know it was a possibility. Given the big changes in his dad's life, maybe the same was happening for his brother and the guy had moved on from his anger at Nick. For all Nick knew, Brandon was ready to shake on a fresh start too. *I sure hope so.*

They sipped their bourbons and then Nick noticed a small brown-and-white dog with long, furry, floppy ears running around outside in the big fenced yard, chasing a squirrel to a tree, which brought to mind Brooke and the twins. He wondered if they were watching those squirrels she'd mentioned. "Who's that?"

"Ah, that's Fritz. He's a cocker spaniel. Wonderful little guy." With absolute joy on his face, his dad watched the dog zipping through the yard, sniffing away, his ears flopping.

Thank you, Cathy Wylie, Nick thought, his guard lowering just a bit—and man, did even that tiny bit feel good. *You've turned my dad around in a great way— that's for sure.*

Jeb's smile faded. "Your mom always wanted a dog and I always said they were too much work, too much trouble. But that was wrong. Dogs are good companions and they're fun to watch. They need people and we need dogs."

Nick heard the catch in his father's voice. He put a hand on his father's shoulder, and they just stood there for a moment, watching Fritz stare up at the squirrel, which was safe on a high, leafy branch.

They might not be talking about the past, but maybe they didn't have to. Maybe they could just let bygones be bygones and start new, like his dad said he wanted. That would be just fine with Nick.

A door opened and shut, and Nick turned to see

his brother glaring at him as he came in the room and headed for the bar.

"Well, well, look who's back," Brandon said. "The prodigal son."

Brandon hadn't changed at all in the five years since Nick had seen him last. His brother had always run five miles a day and worked out four times a week, and he was as fit as ever, his dark hair corporate cut, his suit and shiny black shoes pristine. Nick couldn't see that scrawny, sobbing fourteen-year-old anymore in this guy. Maybe that was a good thing.

"I don't think four tours of duty as a combat soldier for the US Army makes for the prodigal anything," Nick said, leveling a stare at his brother.

Brandon poured himself a bourbon and took a sip of his drink, then continued the glare at Nick. "You had a duty to your family and to the family's bottom line, not to mention future generations of Garroways. But we didn't matter, did we." It was stated, not asked.

Let it go, he told himself. Dad did, and Brandon would too.

"And poor Mom, God rest her soul—" Brandon began.

There it was. There it always was.

"Brandon, that's enough," their father snapped. "Nick's home for good and we're celebrating that. I've invited him to dinner tomorrow night."

He caught the flash of anger in his brother's eyes, then something like...sadness before the anger was back. But for a second Nick did see that fourteen-year-old boy, shaking and screaming, devastated over the loss of their mother. Needing someone to blame, an outlet for his anger. Nick had been able to take it, to bear the heart-wrenching brunt, but there'd been a cost beyond losing his family. He knew that then and he knew it now. When the most important people in your life made you dispensable, you learned to deal with it however you had to.

Nick finished his drink and set down the glass. "Congratulations, Dad. I need to get going, but maybe I'll see you tomorrow night. I need to check my schedule."

"What schedule?" Brandon scoffed. "Give me a break."

Check your temper, Nick reminded himself. "I've taken a temporary job. I need to check with my boss."

"If you worked for Garroway Paper," Brandon said, "You wouldn't have to check with the boss. You'd *be* the boss. Well, co-boss."

He ignored Brandon and turned to his dad, putting a hand on his shoulder. "I'll let you know, Dad. And... thank you." With that, he headed to the door, needing to put some space between himself and his antagonistic brother.

Given Brandon's attitude, Nick had no idea if he'd show up tomorrow night for dinner. If he could, Nick would drive straight out of Wedlock Creek and put this town behind him again.

But he couldn't. He'd made a commitment—to Brooke and to Will Parker—so he was here till August, which meant he'd have to deal with Brandon whether he liked it or not. He definitely did not like it. But he'd learned in the army—and at the base rehab—that the only way forward was to actually embrace the hardship in order to come out ahead. He'd have to deal with his brother head-on.

Suddenly all he wanted was to be at Brooke's house, surrounded by her and those cute babies and the black-and-white cats. Strange as it was there, and as strange as his job title sounded to his own ears, being at Brooke's had somehow become his haven.

Chapter Four

Brooke could tell that something was bothering Nick, something that *wasn't* bothering him before he went to see his dad. The two of them were sitting at the kitchen table, eating the amazing chili and corn bread Nick had made. Of course the man cooked. She barely knew Nick Garroway, but she would not be exaggerating by calling him a domestic god. He didn't look the part; he looked more like he should be on a horse or out patrolling the streets. But he sure *was* the part.

I have a manny, she thought, smiling to herself. *Oh, that's my manny*, she imagined herself saying if someone asked who the hunk holding her twins was. *Meet my manny*. She almost laughed out loud at how crazy it sounded to her own ears.

Well, Nick Garroway might be the twins' new

manny, but she loved bath time and readying the babies for bed with fresh pajamas and stories, so she'd insisted on taking care of that, and he'd unexpectedly made them dinner. To come downstairs to the aroma of chili almost made her think she'd dreamed this whole arrangement. When was the last time someone had cooked for her? He'd even set out the cloth napkins. She'd forgotten she actually had those.

"Everything go okay at your dad's?" she'd dared to ask, not sure if she was prying.

He pushed his chili around on the plate. "Yes and no." She almost lost her appetite as he explained how his father and brother thought he'd betrayed them by enlisting in the army instead of working toward a business degree and joining Garroway Paper, and how his brother had explicitly blamed him for making his frail mother sicker. How his relationship with his father and brother had never recovered from that. "But now he's engaged to a yoga teacher who appreciates the origin of paper, and I guess happiness and her more zen qualities rubbed off on him, because he practically welcomed me home with open arms. He even invited me to dinner tomorrow night."

Her mouth dropped open and she felt her eyes going wide. "Wait a minute. My prospective new client is a yoga instructor. She invited me to dinner tomorrow night, at her fiancé's house, to meet the two of them and discuss plans." She grabbed her phone and checked her calendar for the note she'd made. "Is your father's address 249 Applewood Road?"

He smiled but seemed hardly surprised. That was life

in a small town. "Guess you'll be seeing where I grew up. Oh, and you'll meet my brother, who hates me."

"*Hates* you? That's a pretty strong word."

Nick nodded, his blue eyes narrowing. "Trust me. He does. Over a decade later, he still blames me for my mother's death."

You'd never know it from Nick's expression, but somehow she could tell that he was deeply affected by it and had been all those years. She wondered if he blamed himself too. She sure hoped not.

He dug into his chili and barely looked up, so she sensed he wanted to change the conversation, that maybe he'd decided he'd said too much. She took a piece of his delicious corn bread and lathered it with butter. Pure comfort.

"Feel free to make corn bread every single day," she said. "It's so good."

He smiled. "Army cook's recipe. I begged for it. I've never been much of a cook, but I had to know how to make Doogie's chili and corn bread. You'll soon see that my chef skills are limited to about five basic dishes."

"Eating home-cooked food that I don't have to make when I can't afford to get takeout?" she said. "Sounds very good to me."

He eyed her, then took a piece of corn bread himself. "Dream Weddings isn't doing well?"

Brooke frowned, her appetite disappearing for good. "Well, it's not what it was when my grandmother was here. She *was* Dream Weddings. Everyone knew Aggie Timber and she knew everyone. My gram was very warm and friendly, a real schmoozer, the type who'd talk to the person behind her and in front of her in line at the grocery store. I'm on the quieter side and kind of shy. I don't have her larger-than-life personality."

"Do you need that to plan someone's dream wedding, though?"

"No. But sometimes I wish I were more like her. One of my competitors is. She's raking in a lot of new engagements. And weddings are a big tourist draw here in Wedlock Creek, as I'm sure you know."

"Because of the chapel, right? Some legend about multiples?"

She nodded, picturing the beautiful century-old white chapel in the center of town. "According to the legend, those who marry at the chapel will have multiples in some way, shape or form, whether through luck, science, marriage or happenstance."

He nodded. "Not sure I believe in the legend, but we definitely have a lot of multiples in Wedlock Creek. Including your two."

"And I didn't even get married in the chapel. Or at all," she added. She hadn't figured on getting pregnant at twenty-five and turning twenty-six as a single mother. But as her gram always said, *Expect the unexpected.* It was Aggie Timber's motto for running her business. *You plan an outdoor wedding and the big day arrives, raining cats and dogs. What's the plan B? Always have a plan B and you're fine.*

In Brooke's case, a plan B for how to raise twins without a husband, or any family at all, was to *make* family: good friends, good neighbors, good nanny. But Brooke's two closest friends had moved out of town before her grandmother had died, and her neighbors were busy with their own lives and their own children. So what was left was a good nanny. And right now, thanks to Nick, she had that.

"Have you planned a lot of weddings at the chapel?" he asked.

"It's split half and half. Some couples want nothing to do with multiple babies at once. Some hope for quadruplets." She smiled. "Anyway, I like believing in legends and magic and fate and all that, so I'm a sucker for the legend. Something is definitely in the water in Wedlock Creek. We have more multiples here than just about anywhere. So brides from far away who believe in the legend hire wedding planners in town. I've had clients from all over the country."

"Well, I have no doubt my dad's fiancé will sign with you instead of your chattier competition. I hear you have an in with the son of the groom." He grinned, and for a moment she lost herself in the way his entire handsome face lit up. But then his expression darkened, as if remembering that being the son of the groom came with its own problems.

"I just realized something, Nick. The dinner with your dad and Cathy is work for me, so I'll need my manny to watch the twins. But my manny needs to be at the dinner too."

"Let's bring them. Babies have a way of calming people down."

"Or enraging them with their cries and poop explosions. You witnessed that firsthand."

He laughed and ate the last of his chili. "That's a good point. I'll ask my dad. He loves babies, so I'm sure it's no problem."

The doorbell rang, and Brooke headed over to answer

it just as a cry came from upstairs. She waited a heart-beat to see if Mikey would self-soothe back to sleep. But the cry came louder. Then louder.

The doorbell likely hadn't woken up Mikey, but Brooke was struck by the notion that she could actually answer the door, because Nick was heading up the steps to check on the screecher. By the time Brooke pulled open the door, the crying stopped, which meant Nick had Mikey in his arms and was sitting with him in the glider.

On the doorstep were two of her nosiest neighbors, one from across street and one from two houses down on that side, standing there with strange smiles and peering past her.

"Evening, Brooke," said Amy Landon. The middle-aged redhead gazed past Brooke's shoulder as if expecting a naked man to be standing there. "We heard you have a new male nanny—a *live-in*—so we thought we'd come say hi and meet him so we know who's coming and going from your house."

Her gram used to call Amy their own personal Mrs. Kravitz—a real busybody.

"Someone said he looks like he's part of a motor-cycle gang," Erica Jarello added, also peering past her.

Brooke almost smiled at that one. She was more likely to envision Nick on a horse, working cattle, but she could see him in a black leather jacket, revving a Harley. Oh yes, she could.

"Nick," she called behind her. "Some neighbors would love to meet you."

He came down the stairs with Mikey, bright-eyed and holding a little finger puppet, propped up in his arms.

"Hello," he said with a smile to the women. "I'm Nick Garroway. You know Mikey, of course."

Brooke watched both women stare up at him, practically licking their lips. The man was unusually attractive—she'd attest to that. Tall and lean and muscular in those low-slung dark jeans and a blue T-shirt.

Amy feigned interest in the baby for a second before dashing her eyes back up to Nick. "That little sweetie—of course, we do," she said, then introduced herself and Erica before Brooke could even get a word in. Both their hands lingered in Nick's for the handshake. "We live just across the street."

"It's very nice to meet you both." A high-pitched shriek came from upstairs. "Ah, that's Morgan, who just discovered he's alone in the nursery," Nick said. "I'd better go check on the little guy."

Brooke would swear both women literally swooned. Of course, it would be all over town the minute she closed the door behind them that Brooke Timber had a male nanny. Tongues would begin wagging about whether or not they were "involved." Fine, let them talk. Brooke, meanwhile, would enjoy her home-cooked chili and corn bread, and the novelty of watching someone with rippled muscles changing diapers and playing peekaboo with her children. If the neighbors would begin wondering if something was going on between them, Brooke herself would enjoy thinking about that very subject too. She might not be remotely interested in anything to do with romance—men said one thing and then did another—but fantasizing about kissing Nick? No harm there. It wasn't like she'd ever *do* it. Look But Don't Touch was a motto for a reason.

Amy and Erica peered behind Brooke again, clearly hoping for something juicy to see or hear to spread around the neighborhood, but there was no sign of the manny. They smiled at Brooke, and Amy said, "Well, that's sure a change from the usual!" and then the two women finally turned and left.

Nick came back downstairs, this time with Morgan in his arms. "Mikey's eyes drooped halfway up the stairs. He's asleep again. This one?" he said, hoisting up Morgan. "He got lonely up there by himself and asked me for a story, so I'll tell him one about the time a lizard tried to steal my lunch and then put him back down."

"Oh, he asked for a story, did he?" Brooke said with a smile.

"I can read him. Mikey too. For example, just before, Mikey made it clear he wanted a back rub, so I gave him one before laying him down and wham—asleep."

"*How* are you so good with them?" Brooke asked in wonder.

He shrugged. "Probably because I'm just passing through. Novelty makes everything easy and fun. Doesn't it." Statement, not a question.

Damn straight it did. Will Parker's good-looking face appeared in her mind. She'd been a novelty to him and he'd made her feel like she was everything. But he'd just been passing through too.

Nick might as well have dumped a bucket of cold water on her head. Then again, that was a good thing. She needed to keep being reminded that he wasn't her fantasy come to life. He wasn't the man of her dreams. The man of her dreams wasn't just passing through. And anyway, there *was* no man of her dreams, because she didn't believe in any of that anymore. People did one thing and said another. Said one thing and did another. She could only trust herself. Once burned so badly, a million times shy.

And with her life, there was no room for anything but what was already there: her children and her business.

"About the neighbors," Nick said, gesturing toward the door. "Is my living here going to be a problem for you?"

"Tongues wagging?" Brooke asked. "Let them. I'm used to being the focus of gossip. I went from being single, quiet Brooke to suddenly being visibly pregnant and, boy, did that spark a lot of gossip. I actually overheard one of the neighbors who was at the door, talking about me in Java Jane's one day, wondering who the father was and if he'd abandoned me." She shook her head. "I wanted to poke my head around the column blocking me from view and say, 'Why, yes he did, Amy.'" All that old hurt and embarrassment—more at her own stupidity for falling for all that nonsense Will had sputtered—came over her, and she crossed her arms over her chest.

"Happens to the best of us," he said.

She eyed him. "Including you?"

"Including me—for the craziest reasons that often have nothing to do with us. Know what I mean?"

She shrugged. "That it's not always personal? If that's what you mean, sorry but it's baloney. It's always personal. I wasn't this or that enough."

"To one particular guy, at one particular time," he said. "In the space-and-time continuum, Brooke, you're *everything*."

"The space-and-time what?" She laughed. "I have no idea what you mean and totally do at the same time."

"I'm just saying that *everyone* gets hurt. Victoria's Secret supermodels. The Pope. Little kids. No one is immune, no matter how gorgeous or how good or innocent. And it very often has nothing to do with you and everything to do with someone else. No immunity."

"Including you," she said with a bit of a prompt in her tone, hoping he'd elaborate on his own love troubles.

But he didn't. Rats. She wanted to know the juicy details. Plus she wondered who his type was, what kind of woman could win his heart.

"Yeah," was all he said, then did a one-handed peek-aboo with Morgan. "I see you," he said in a singsong way to the baby, who gurgled happily at him.

I want to know more about you, she thought. *I want to know everything about you.*

But she didn't want to pry. If he wanted to talk about his ex, he would. She certainly didn't want to talk about hers.

"I think this little one is ready for bed again," he said. "There's another big yawn. Tell you what, Brooke. Let's me settle him back in his crib and then I'll take care of the kitchen."

"I'll put him back," she said, reaching for him. "I know I need a nanny for when I'm working, but I'm certainly not working right now." She cuddled Morgan in her arms, kissing his baby-shampoo-scented hair. "Giving them their baths, putting on their pj's, snuggling them as I read a story in the nursery, then laying their sleepy little bodies in their cribs. Every night, when I do that and then just watch their eyes start to close, I feel like I have everything."

She sighed inwardly. There she went again, saying too much, making herself look…needy. She didn't want to come across that way.

"Well, you do have everything," he said.

That made her wonder. He'd said he wasn't the marrying kind. Or the father kind. And yet, because she had Morgan and Mikey, this sweet little family of three, he considered that *everything*. There was a contradiction there. Or maybe just ambivalence.

It doesn't matter, she reminded herself. *You're not looking for holes in his story about who he is*. And was there anything worse than ambivalence?

"So, you go put Morgan back to sleep, and I'll straighten up in the kitchen. Then we'll meet in the living room and talk about my schedule and what you'd like me to handle, and you can give me the grand tour of the house."

Part of her was glad to escape him again—he listened too intently, looked at her too closely, inferred too well. The other part never wanted to be more than a foot away from him.

Fifteen minutes later—Morgan needed a story and a little rocking to fall back asleep—Brooke came downstairs to find the dishwasher going and the kitchen spotless. In the living room was a pitcher of iced tea that he must have made and a plate of the mixed cookies she'd picked up yesterday, unable to resist anything from the Solero Sisters bakery. The man was amazing. Every woman should have one of him.

"Army taught you all this?" she asked in complete

wonder. "Making a kitchen spotless? Whipping up iced tea with lemon wedges?" she asked. Or had a previous live-in love? An ex-wife? An ex-girlfriend? She doubted he'd been married before. But he'd hinted at an ex. She was *so* curious.

"Not so much how to clean a kitchen counter or load a dishwasher," he said, "but to take care of business. Do what needs doing, the right way and efficiently, and it's done. A little initiative is all it takes to learn how to do something—and correctly."

Did he have any idea what an aphrodisiac this kind of talk was to her? Someone she could trust to take care of stuff? Without her even asking? "It sure is nice to have you around, Nick Garroway."

He smiled—that big, sexy smile that made her knees wobble. "I'm glad one person in this town feels that way."

She reached out and touched his shoulder, which was hard, muscular and broad, and he looked at her for a moment. Uh oh. She quickly pulled her hand away. He was attracted to her; she could tell. And if it wasn't obvious, now he knew she was attracted to him too. Dammit. She needed that to be a secret. From him.

"About that work schedule," she said, clearing her throat and moving into the living room, trying to be all business.

But he poured her a glass of iced tea and nudged the cookie plate toward her, and she felt so taken care of that again she just wanted to run with it and lay her head against his chest, feel his arms around her. Just for a few moments, even. Ever since her grandmother had passed away, and then she had found out she was pregnant, she'd had to tell herself that everything was going to be okay. In Nick's company, she *believed* it.

She took a sip of the iced tea, so refreshing and perfectly sweet and lemony. He sat just a foot away from her on the sofa, angled toward her, and again she was struck by the urge to lay her head in his lap and have him stroke her hair. Or to kiss him hard on the lips. She sat back, so aware of him. Brooke was five foot seven, so not exactly petite, but Nick towered over her.

To distract herself from him, she started talking about the ideal schedule for her, and of course he said that whatever worked for her worked for him, since his whole point in taking the job was to be of help to her. They decided on a similar schedule that her former nanny had. He'd do overnight wake-ups so that she wouldn't be bleary-eyed during the day while working on weddings and dealing with bridezillas—her New Year's Eve–client was one of those. She'd care for the twins from 5:00 a.m. to 9:00 a.m., for breakfast and playtime, and then he'd take over from 9:00 a.m. to 1:00 p.m., including on Saturdays, which was always a busy workday, and again between 5:00 p.m. and 6:00 p.m., when for some reason her brides tended to panic most. Sunday would be a complete day off for him—unless she needed him to watch the babies because of a crazed client or wedding emergency. In fact, he'd added, he would be on call all day, all night.

"I'm here for you," he said—quite seriously.

What was that famous question by Sigmund Freud? What did women want? Brooke Timber wanted someone there for her. Someone in her corner, someone who had her back. Someone she could count on. Trust. Until August, that someone was Nick Garroway.

"And I mean it," he added. "Let's say you get a call that the caterer can't switch the hip sole for the dull salmon and you have to find a new caterer the night before the wedding. Text me and *poof*—" he snapped his fingers "—I'm in the nursery. That simple."

He had no idea how much that made her want to lean over and kiss him. Full on the lips.

He was becoming way too indispensable—in every possible area of her life. But Nick *would* only be here for another couple of weeks. She had to remember that.

"I appreciate that. Very much," she said. "Thank you."

"My pleasure," he said.

Because she could barely handle being so close to him on the couch, she took him on a tour of the small house. The cozy living room, the sunny kitchen and the Dream Weddings office made up the first floor. Three bedrooms on the second floor—the nursery, her room and the guest room, which was his bedroom. She peered in to see his big green duffel bag on the bed. Tonight he'd be in that bed.

There was no way she'd get any sleep knowing that Even if she didn't have to get up to take care of her own children.

Just after midnight Nick heard a cry and got out of his very comfortable bed in the guest room in Brooke's house. He hadn't been sleeping anyway. He'd been thinking about Brooke. All about her.

He kept seeing her face—all her different expressions. Concentration, curiosity, frustration, surprise, contentment. Contentment was usually when she was holding one of her babies. And when she discovered he'd taken care of something she hadn't yet gotten to—changing a lightbulb, scooping the litter box, replenishing the diaper stack in the nursery from the huge bag in the garage. Putting together that bookcase for the nursery. He'd just walked around the house while she'd been working earlier tonight, checked things out and he'd done what needed to be done, whether or not it was baby related. The way he saw it, taking care of the babies meant taking care of their home too. And their mom—their beautiful, sexy mom.

He headed out of his room just as Brooke was coming out of hers. She wore yoga pants, with a long T-shirt and furry slippers, and her hair was in a high ponytail.

"I've got this," he said, wagging a finger at her. "It's my job."

She smiled and slapped a palm to her forehead. "I heard Morgan cry and just popped out of bed without thinking. I forgot I had help."

Morgan let out another shriek, and they smiled at each other and both headed into the nursery.

"I know I could be getting back into bed and blissfully going to back to sleep," she said, "but I guess it's just instinct to want to make sure he's okay. Tired as I always am, I like cuddling the twins in this chair, rocking them back to sleep. I always want them to know everything will be okay."

"I get it. You're looking out for them, and I'm looking out for you."

She smiled. "Is that why I was saved from scooping cat poop earlier?"

He nodded. "If you're not doing those kinds of chores, you're freed up to spend quality time with Morgan and Mikey."

"Yup, I thought it before and now I'll say it aloud—everyone needs one of you."

As she crossed in front of the window, where a sliver of moonlight shone through, she was silhouetted and he was struck—again—by how beautiful she was. He had a sudden yearning to touch her, feel her hair, her face, her lips.

None of the above was why he was here, though, so he tried to focus on the baby fussing. But once they had reached the crib, Morgan had stopped crying; perhaps the voices had lulled him back to sleep. They crept back out of the room and stood in the dim lighting of the hallway.

He had to prolong this. Anything to keep her from turning and disappearing into her bedroom. He wanted to talk to her, look at her, drink her in.

He was surprised by how much too. After Elena and the way she'd blindsided him, he thought he was done with women, done with it all. Now here he was, unable to take his eyes off Brooke, the pull of her too strong.

Then again, he had thought another baby couldn't possibly grip his heartstrings and yank, and the Timber twins were doing just that.

"Well, good night again," she said.

Well, hell. He was about to suggest making some hot chocolate—with marshmallows. Or maybe a game of backgammon, not that he remembered how to play, but he'd seen a set on the coffee table. Or they could watch an old movie.

Except Brooke had to work tomorrow and so did he. If he had to get up a few times a night with the twins, he'd better sleep when he had the chance or he'd be no good to anyone.

Rats. "From now on," he said, "burrow right back under the covers if you hear one of the twins in the middle of the night. I've got it."

"I'll try." She glanced up at him, shaking her head with a smile. "Are you even real?"

"Here," he said, taking her hand and putting it on his cheek. "Real?"

He hadn't meant to do that.

She held his gaze, and parts of him he'd suppressed for months came back to life.

Then suddenly they were kissing and he wasn't even sure who leaned closer to whose lips first. Her hands were on his back, his shoulders and then his hair as they deepened the kiss, and his were inching under her long T-shirt, higher and higher until he felt bare skin. He felt her shudder and he drew her closer.

"Waaah! Waah-waah!"

Noooo. He never wanted this—warmth and magic and sensation—to end.

"Waah-waah!"

"That's Mikey this time," she whispered against his ear. "And a good thing too, because this is crazy." She stepped back and crossed her arms over her chest. "We can't do this, Nick. I can't do this. For many reasons."

And he could probably list them right here. She'd been hurt pretty badly by Parker—that went without saying. Her trust level was probably at an all-time low. Plus she had enough on her plate without adding a love affair with her live-in manny to the mix. Her *temporary* live-in manny.

Plus he'd said it himself. He wasn't a family guy. She was a family woman, a package deal. So he'd better keep his lips and hands and mind off her.

And anyway, tomorrow night they'd be having dinner at his dad's house. With his brother running his mouth. Nick had no doubt he'd need all his focus on getting through the meal without making a fist.

He headed back to his room, one of the black-and-white cats—Smudge, he thought—padding up the stairs and stopping in front of his doorway. The cat stared at him with narrowed green eyes, as if shaking his furry head at him. *Hands off the woman*, he was pretty sure Smudge was telling him, but then the cat went into his room and jumped on the bed, making himself comfortable. A few seconds later, Snowball joined him.

If he had to be honest, he was glad for the company. Nick had become something of a loner over the years—lately in particular—but he didn't like being alone. Not at all.

We can't do this, Nick. I can't do this, for many reasons...

Listen to the cat. No more touching Brooke—no matter how badly he wanted or needed to.

Chapter Five

As if she could sleep after that. Brooke did close her eyes; every moment was committed to memory. The way his lips felt, his hands on her, the pure desire she'd felt. If Mikey hadn't cried, she might have taken his hand and led him to her bedroom, and that would have been a huge mistake. Not in the immediate short-term maybe; in fact, despite *everything*, sleeping with a man who looked like Nick Garroway struck her as exactly what she needed, the way a double espresso or two glasses of wine or a big slice of chocolate cake could have an immediate impact.

But in the morning—the awkwardness. The weird thing they'd have to do to get back to a professional relationship. Even if—and it was a big even *if*—Brooke was willing to let herself fall for another man, she was under no illusions that Nick was going to fall magically in love and become a family man just because he had the moves.

Put him out of your mind, she told herself. *You're wide awake, so you might as well get some work done.* She grabbed her laptop and opened up the Satler file. Soon she had pages filled of options, graphics of how they would complement one another, such as table settings and centerpieces, wedding gowns and bridal party dresses, caterers, bakers, and three individual wedding cakes that worked together yet fit each sister in a particular way. And of course, how each bride could feel it was *her* day, rather than *their* day, in a triple extravaganza. She'd give it a polish in the morning, then email the Satlers, pretty confident they'd hire her.

Her email icon lit up, and Brooke clicked it. Her New Year's Eve–bride, Francesca, was obsessing over what to do at midnight.

Should we have the ceremony start at midnight, or should the minister time the "I now pronounce you husband and wife" at midnight? Or should just the kiss come at midnight? Thoughts?

Francesca ended the email with a stressed-face emoticon.

If Brooke knew her more-than-slightly neurotic client, Francesca, and she did, she had a very strong hunch that Francesca had picked a fight with Bryce, her salt-of-the-earth fiancé, because she was anxious about something else entirely, and that anxiety had morphed into obsessing over tiny details of her midnight wedding, six months from now. All she really had to do here was remind Francesca of what Francesca really needed at that moment.

No matter what you choose, you're marrying the man you love, the man of your dreams, the guy who sat beside you in the emergency vet's office at 3:00 a.m. last winter when that sweet boxer of yours had been injured. Just marry him. Everything else is icing. I love the idea of ceremony starting at the stroke of midnight—your first instinct when we sat down to plan out your wedding.

She clicked about ten different emojis, including a wedding gown, a top hat, two hearts, a man and a woman facing each other with lips pursed, and clicked send.

You are so right, Brooke! I knew I could count on you—even at 3:17 a.m.!

If only life were always this easy, Brooke thought, sending back a smiley face and then shutting off her laptop.

But she still couldn't sleep. All she could think about was that story Francesca had told her about her beloved dog getting hurt in the middle of the night when he went through the doggie door, into the yard, and found some preying animal out there, and she'd called her then-boyfriend, now-fiancé, sobbing and scared. He'd rushed over, gotten her into his car, gently wrapped the dog in a towel and rushed him over to the emergency vet, a half hour away, then handled every-thing, from talking to the vet to the medications to the bill. The kicker? Her boyfriend didn't like dogs and didn't want a dog, and hers had been a huge argument between them since they'd met a month prior, since he didn't want to come over to her place and hated how the dog's schedule determined hers. They'd been on the verge of breaking up.

But when Francesca was sobbing and scared, and the dog needed help? He was there. With everything he had. That night taught them both something about how they felt. Two months later: engaged.

That was what Brooke *really* wanted: someone she could call at 2:00 a.m., someone who'd rush over. Someone she could count on. Through her pregnancy and since the twins were born, she'd been on her own through it all, the scary moments, the joyous moments. She'd thought she was done with love, but the truth was that she wanted her person so badly, her heart hurt. But at the same time, she wasn't exactly in trust mode. Since her grandmother had died, Brooke had felt something of a crusty shell forming over her, inside her. Not hard-ened, exactly, but there.

She temporarily had Nick Garroway, who was so there for her, she almost couldn't process it. *There for me...until August.* Then poof, gone. Like Will Parker.

Tears stung her eyes, and she took a breath and fo-cused on the faces of her twins. Everything she did, she did for them. She saw their dimples and their soft brown hair, those big blue-hazel eyes that the pedia-trician said would probably turn her own pale brown shade in a couple of months.

A calm came over her and as she felt herself drifting off to sleep, she thought she heard a baby crying. *Nick's got it*, she thought, burrowing under the quilt as he'd told her to do. But instead of falling asleep in a warm cocoon, everything taken care of, her eyes popped open. Because she'd realized right then that letting Nick handle the 3:30 a.m. wake-up time while she went back to sleep—or tried to—meant that she did *trust* him.

There was basic trust, and then there was this deep sense of peace she felt in her bones about Nick Garroway. She had the crazy feeling he'd lay down his life for her and the twins.

But would he stay for her and the twins when he wasn't needed? No way. No matter what that man represented to her between now and August, she couldn't forget that he wasn't ever going to be hers—or be her babies' father.

There was no mention of the kiss the next morning. Nick wanted to bring it up in order to apologize again, but how awkward would that be? Brooke was moving around the house, avoiding whatever room he was in—and eye contact. Okay, fine, she needed some space from what had happened and so did he. He'd tried to sleep but couldn't, so he took a long, hot shower and got dressed, then checked out the *Gazette* online to see what was happening in town for kids and babies. Bingo: story time at the library for babies through eighteen months.

At exactly nine o'clock on the dot, he was about to head into the kitchen when he heard Brooke telling the twins a story about Grammy Aggie, and he was so touched that, for a moment, he held back and listened.

"Grammy Aggie was a magical nana who made everyone feel special," she was saying. "She had two kitty assistants, named Snowball and Smudge. One day Grammy Aggie's own granddaughter, a little girl named Brooke, was sad about not having parents, because a mean girl at school was making fun of her for it, and Grammy Aggie told Brooke that she did have parents, that they were in heaven and were her special guardian angels, just like your father is now."

Nick lowered his head at the mention of Will. He didn't hear the note of bitterness in her voice that had been there yesterday, and he was glad for that. If he did anything in his short time with the Timber family, he was grateful he could give all three of them a little piece of Will Parker back, the best part, the part that did care and had wished he'd acted differently. There were many moments of truth, and in that final one, these three had been loved by Parker.

"Ga ba ga!" one of the babies said. Nick could easily tell the twins apart physically, but he didn't have their babbles down yet.

"Ga ba ga!" Brooke said back and laughed, and one of the babies laughed, the sweetest sound on earth.

He figured it was safe to come in. The babies were in their swings, on the table.

She glanced up at him and then hid her face in a mug of coffee. "Morning," she mumbled.

"About that kiss," he said, then mentally whacked himself upside the head. Hadn't he just told himself it would be awkward to talk about it? They'd covered it night last—the kiss had been a mistake that wouldn't happen again. End of story.

Except things were awkward regardless right now and ignoring reality had never really worked out for Nick. It was his go-to, to just pretend certain issues didn't bother him when they were tearing his gut apart. He didn't want to do that with Brooke.

"Nothing to talk about," she said brightly, shutting her laptop. "Great news—I spent a good hour last night finalizing the Satler plans and sent it off before the twins even woke up this morning. Cross your fingers for me. Dream Weddings needs their triple business."

Well then. He'd tried. Perhaps he should just let it go.

"I'm sure they'll hire you, Brooke. Didn't one say you were 99 percent hired?"

She smiled. "Thanks to my manny." Her cheeks turned red. "Are you okay with being referred to as a manny? I could call you a nanny or a sitter."

"Manny, nanny, sitter. All good." He smiled, then glanced at the clock. "Ah, time to get to the library. It's baby hour. There's a story time for crawlers. For babies up to a year and a half."

"You want to go to that? I went once and wow, the noise. Between the shrieking and the crying and the crawler who pulled up on my knee and then spit up on me, I haven't been back."

Nick smiled. "Well, it sounds like my kind of event. I figured on that and then a stroll back here for tummy time, rest hour and then lunch."

She tilted her head and stared at him. "How do you know about tummy time?"

"It's my job to know." Plus he'd done a lot of research in those couple of hours after the kiss, when he hadn't been able to sleep. He'd gotten a crash course on three-month-old babies and read up on twins too.

She stared at him so hard, he would pay to know what she was thinking.

"Well, I'd love to come," she said. "Not being the sole responsible party for them at crowded baby events makes it lot more fun. And I'm all done with work for the day, until the meeting tonight with my new client and your dad."

Oh right. That. At least the question of whether or not he was going was taken out of the equation. He *had* to go for his new job. "I was trying to put that out of my head."

"Oh. Sorry. Is it really that bad?"

He nodded. "Well, at least not where my dad is concerned, so that's something. Maybe a happy occasion like a wedding will help my brother's mind-set. It's definitely helped my father."

She seemed about to ask a question about his family, so he rushed to mention he wanted to change the twins before they left, then dashed them upstairs.

Once back down, they each put a twin in the stroller, packed up the stroller bag and off they went.

Nosy Amy waved from her porch, where she was sitting on a white rocking chair and reading the *Gazette*, with a yellow mug on the little table next to her. As they crossed the street, she called out, "You look just like a family!"

Every muscle in Nick's body seized up, and he felt Brooke stiffen beside him.

He shot Amy a tight smile, noticing Brooke doing the same.

"Busybody!" Brooke whisper-muttered.

The woman continued to stare at them as they made their way toward Main Street.

"You just know she thinks we're involved," Brooke said. "She's probably spreading rumors all over town."

"We should make out in front of her," Nick said. "*Really* give her something to talk about."

Brooke grinned. "You're right. Why do I even let her get to me?"

"You're human. Can't be helped."

"It's really nice having someone on my team," she said. "I miss that more than anything."

"Your grandmother?" he asked. "I heard a little of the Grammy Aggie story you were telling the twins."

She glanced at him. "My gram and my friends who moved. I got used to being so alone and didn't realize how much I missed having people there for me. Even just people to diss Amy on my behalf."

"Oh, I'm happy to help there. Team Brooke, all the way."

She looked at him again, then kept her gaze straight ahead. "That promise you made really means something to you, doesn't it."

"Yes. It does."

She nodded slowly. It suddenly struck him that she thought *that* was what he was talking about, that that was why he was here, doing all this. It was and wasn't. The promise had brought him to her house, but Brooke had taken over in importance; it was *Brooke* who had him bending over backward, not a promise he'd made to the man who'd saved his life.

But there was no need to tell her that, and it was better that she didn't know. He wasn't sure *he* wanted to know. Still, somehow, when it came to Brooke, things were clear.

You look just like a family... Once upon a time, very briefly, he'd thought that about himself and another woman and a baby, but he'd quickly learned he'd been romanticizing, that he didn't share Elena's strong feelings so much as he was attracted to her and believed in the aid work she was doing at an Afghan orphanage. His heart had really only belonged to little Aisha, just a few months old. In the end he'd hurt Elena and destroyed his opportunity to keep tabs on the baby he'd found abandoned near their unit.

He'd screwed up so hard that, for a solid few weeks, he'd questioned every judgment he made and worried about the soldiers around him. Slowly he'd gotten himself back and tried not to think about Elena or Aisha, but he wasn't about to make the same mistake with Brooke and her twins. He was attracted, yes. He felt responsible for her and her children. But his heart had long been buried under rough scar tissue.

No more kisses in the middle of the night, he told himself. He glanced at her in her tank top and denim skirt and sandals and sparkly blue toenails. No matter how much he wanted Brooke Timber in his bed, being physically involved never came without emotional shackles. And unless he could imagine walking down Main Street with Brooke and her children as more than just the nanny—manny—he had to do something about his attraction to her.

Like ignore it. He wouldn't be part of her family or his own. That word had been blown to bits for him by the Garroways. But then Elena had envisioned exactly that—a family—of her, him and the baby girl who'd brought them together. He'd hurt Elena, and she'd been furious, and she'd shut him out of the baby's life. That was over a year ago and he was still surprised at how much it stung. In the end it was for the best, of course, but it still burned a hole in his gut.

He shut his eyes against the memories. As a soldier, he'd been trained to ignore everything but the mission. He'd simply take over as his own commander. Brooke Timber was off-limits and that was an order.

They turned onto Main Street and headed into the library, which easily snapped him out of the past. The children's room was crowded with parents and caregivers and lots of babies, both crawling and in strollers. Unfortunately story time meant sitting on the floor, and since he was a big guy, he chose spots in the back of the room. With the stroller parked, he and Brooke both took a twin and sat on the floor with a baby in their laps.

"Let me see those darling little Timber twins!" a middle-aged blonde woman sitting diagonally said as she scooted closer. "Aren't they adorable. What sweet cheeks! And look at those dimples!"

Nick was waiting for the lady to take a breath, but she kept going with her comments. At least she was being nice.

"You two are being good for Mommy and Daddy, aren't you!" the woman continued, tapping each baby on the nose.

For the second time in fifteen minutes, Nick froze. Daddy? Him? Nick thought he radiated "not a father" but then again, he *was* the manny.

"Actually, Natalie—" Brooke started to say, but Mikey started shrieking.

"Oh, you little cutie," Natalie cut in. "So temperamental. Well, better get back to my spot before someone takes it. Nice to see you!" After making the baby cry, she hurried off.

Nick scowled at her back, but story time was starting, so he kept his thoughts to himself.

Like that he'd been mistaken for Brooke's husband and the twins' father. He hoisted Mikey high in his arms and rubbed his back, and that ended the shrieks. The little guy wasn't exactly listening to the librarian with the melodic voice read a Curious George book or looking at the pictures she held up high, but at least he was quiet now.

As the hour ended and they left in a sea of toddlers and strollers, Brooke was quiet.

"Dollar for your thoughts," he said as they exited the library and stepped into the brilliant July sunshine.

"Worth that much? When we were kids, it was a penny."

"And no one ever got that penny, so I figured that was still the case."

She smiled. "I was just thinking."

"About?"

"About how much I liked Natalie Howaman mistaking us for a family."

"Because you don't like having a male nanny?"

"Because I like the idea of having a husband. A father for the twins. In that twenty seconds of her assumption, I did. And I *really* liked it. I thought I was done with men and dating and romance after Will. But I'm not. I *can't* be. That's giving up. And how can I give up when I have two very young, impressionable people to model life for?"

He stared at her, unsure what to say.

What he wanted to blurt out was, *I'm just the nanny, lady.* But he'd asked, hadn't he?

He knew his discomfort came from feeling responsible for what she'd said. About wanting a husband and father for her children. But that guy couldn't be him.

"I can understand that," he said. "You're a good mother, Brooke."

"That's the most important thing to me."

What was the most important thing to him? Making sure Brooke was okay and then hitting the road, buying the ranch he'd been dreaming of for a long time now.

Yes—that was it. He'd get Brooke settled, her real nanny would return and then he'd leave in peace. He always felt better when he knew, solidly, what he was doing.

"I'm surprised anyone could mistake me for a family man," he said. "Someone once told me I radiated loner." Not that that was a good thing. Elena had been right though. He'd bonded with her, to a point, over baby Aisha's well-being as she'd been nursed back to health, but that bond wasn't all that strong for him, not like it had been for Elena. He wasn't meant to be part of a family. Hadn't that been made clear to her? No, it hadn't.

She glanced at him. "What you radiate, in my now experienced opinion, is 'good with babies.' You said you took care of a baby overseas? In Afghanistan?"

He frowned. The topic was on his mind and she'd

just brought it up, so maybe that was a sign he should tell her. Talking about Elena and Aisha would bring it all back to the surface and remind him of what had happened when he wasn't forthright—even if it wasn't intentional. He absolutely *had* to be with Brooke.

"Yes," he said, that pretty, tiny face with round dark eyes and wispy black hair coming into his mind. "I helped care for a baby for several days during random time off when I was a soldier. I had to learn on the job, and for some reason, a lot of it came naturally."

"I'll push," he said, putting a hand on the stroller bar. He needed something to do.

She stepped to the side, tilting her head as she looked at him. "Whose baby was it?"

Aisha would be a toddler, talking, walking. "I came across an abandoned baby while on patrol outside our unit," he said, wheeling the stroller down the curb and then back up across the street. "She ended up being adopted by an aid worker, so she's fine." He shook his head. "But I wasn't fine—not for a long time."

Brooke stopped walking and put a hand on his arm. "What happened?"

"Let's keep walking," he said. "It helps to be doing something while I talk." *While I think about it.*

As they walked, slowly he told her everything. How he'd found the baby in a rough basket lined with a tattered blanket and a note handwritten in Dari. He'd made out the few words: *orphan, sick, help* and *needs a home*. The words had punched his gut. He could remember looking down into the basket, at the sweet, innocent baby, so helpless and alone and ill. Right then he was all the baby had. He'd left a note, in the basic Dari language he'd picked up, tacked to a nearby tree, that the baby would be at a local orphanage run by aid workers, since they had access to a doctor and nurse there.

The baby had been very sick and no one was sure if she'd pull through. One of the aid workers, Elena, a kind, young American woman from Indiana, named her Aisha, which was Arabic for alive and well, and promised to give her TLC while she was being evaluated and treated. He'd been aware that Elena had a crush on him; she didn't hide it, and he'd been so overwhelmed with emotion that he'd kissed her. And more. But he'd never really been thinking about Elena through any of it. And he regretted that more than anything.

Back then the relief he'd felt, that even if the baby didn't pull through that she'd be loved for her remaining time, had shaken him so much, he'd been oblivious to most else going on. When had he started caring? He'd had two days off and had gone back to see Aisha both days, holding her, rocking her, talking to her, asking her to pull through so that she could find a new family. And when the doctor had reported that Aisha had turned a corner, he'd picked Elena up and swung her around, setting her down with a kiss on the cheek.

Elena hadn't liked the cheek kiss. She could tell right away that something was different between them now that the baby was all right. She'd mistaken his deep concern for Aisha, the little one he'd found, with love for her—Elena.

What a disaster that had turned into. Elena had started talking about adopting Aisha together. She'd thrown the word *marriage* around. How had he gotten this so wrong? How could he not have seen any of this coming? Was he blind? Unable to see what was right in front of him? Maybe he was just selfish, self-absorbed, so used to keeping to himself that there was no room for anyone else in his head. But he'd had to come clean with her, and he had, as gently as he could. Elena had been devastated and had told him to leave.

He'd come back his next day off to be told that Elena was adopting Aisha herself and that he wasn't welcome, that he was a liar and had misled her. He hadn't meant to. Sometimes he'd jar awake at night, thinking about Aisha's big dark eyes, and Elena's anger, hating that he'd hurt her.

He didn't like thinking about it—the baby, the betrayal in Elena's eyes, his regret that he'd unintentionally made her think he had plans for the three of them as a family, even a makeshift one while they were overseas.

Nick knew his limitations.

"I'm glad that Aisha found a good home," Brooke said, stopping again and turning to look at him. "Although it sounds like it was rough going for you, at least that precious baby you rescued is all right now."

He nodded against the lump in his throat and pushed the stroller up the slight incline of the next curb. "That's true." He resumed walking and she did too.

"I hope you keep your thoughts on that," she added. "Instead of where you think you went wrong. You did so much right, so much good, Nick."

He shrugged. "I unintentionally misled someone. And then I got blindsided because of it. I hated being shut out of Aisha's life, not knowing if she was thriving, although I assume she was." He let out a breath and shook his head. "I thought I was pretty closed off before all that—when Elena slammed the orphanage door in my face and told me I wasn't welcome, I felt something else shutter inside me."

"Oh, Nick. I'm so sorry about all that."

He nodded because he'd run out of steam; he didn't want to talk about this anymore.

Because he was dangerously close to doing it all again. By kissing Brooke last night, he'd started down a path he had no plans to continue to go down; he was exiting on a different road in just a couple of weeks. He was buying a ranch, located hours from Wedlock Creek.

He couldn't imagine making Brooke think he had intentions other than to help her out, to be what she needed until her nanny returned. He had to be careful with how he acted, how he presented himself. And kissing her was exactly the way to mess everything up.

He had to be careful. He couldn't hurt Brooke. He wouldn't.

Chapter Six

As Brooke got ready for the dinner with her new client—and Nick's father and brother—she couldn't stop thinking about everything he'd told her. At least now she knew what she was dealing with.

She pulled a sleeveless floral sheath dress from her closet, and a pair of low-heeled sandals, aware of how nice it was to get ready without the twins in their carriers, on her bed. A few weeks ago, with no nanny or sitters available, she'd had to bring the twins with her to the Mayfair Hotel in Brewer for wedding-day prep for the Webber-Hayfield union, and she'd been on the phone with the very late florist when she realized she had two different shoes on. Between the stroller—albeit quiet stroller, thanks to the serious napping her twins had done that late afternoon—and her mismatched shoes and the spit-up on the lapel of her suit, she'd gotten more than a few raised eyebrows and zero referrals from the Webbers or the Hayfields.

She had a lot on her mind right now—Nick, the dinner at his family's home, not to mention hoping to secure his future stepmother as her client—and not having to worry about the twins right now was a relief. She could hear Mikey babbling in the nursery and occasionally Nick's voice as he talked to the twins. He was telling them they were going to get to meet his dad's dog, Fritz, and that he was probably the cutest dog they'd ever seen in their three months on earth.

She laughed, marveling at how Nick always managed to make her forget her stress—even when he was the cause of it.

She froze for a moment, wondering if being with her twins caused *him* stress, reminding him of Aisha and all he'd gone through. He'd walked into her life, picked up Mikey and taken the job as her nanny all to fulfill a promise, so if her babies did trigger memories, he certainly plowed through it. The soldier in him, she realized. But still, what did he do with all of those feelings?

He probably dismissed them. Ignored them. Fought them.

She sat on her bed and slipped her right foot into a flat brown hiking sandal before she realized it hardly matched the pretty silver one on her right foot. She shook her head and kicked off the brown one, then grabbed the other silver one. *Concentrate*, she told herself. *Stop thinking about Nick Garroway when he's not going to be here come August. Appreciate him while he's your hot manny, but stop wondering and speculating...and fantasizing.*

As if she could stop thinking about the way he'd kissed her, how she'd been backed against the wall, his hands roaming, the hard planes of his chest pressed to hers.

"Fritz has the floppiest ears you'll ever see," she heard Nick say.

"Ba ga!" Mikey yelled.

Then baby laughter.

"You little scamp! Does your chewy bunny like being thrown on the floor? I doubt it."

More baby laughter.

She sighed and strapped on the silver sandal. The reality of her life and the fantasy of Nick were one and the same. That was the problem. That was why she couldn't stop the crazy thoughts popping into her mind all day.

You look like a family...

Her family had always been just the three of them—she and the twins. She'd been alone in the delivery room. No husband, no significant other, no family. She'd been alone while pushing the stroller up and down Main Street these past three months, noticing all the families. Not just ones that included two partners, but generations of family. Grandparents, aunts, uncles, cousins. It wasn't her life, but what she'd give for her twins to have all that love and connection and a clan of their own.

"Five minutes to head out," came the loud, strong voice of her hot manny.

Nick Garroway wouldn't let her leave the house with mismatched shoes or baby spit-up on her lapel.

He wouldn't let her be late to a meeting. He was here for her, just like he'd said he'd be.

Like he'd promised to be.

She bit her lip. All those crazy thoughts she was having? She had to stop it. He'd promised a fallen soldier to make sure she was okay, and since she wasn't really okay, he'd stepped into her life and was taking over until her regular nanny returned. *That's all this is*, she reminded herself. *If you forget it for a second, you're an even bigger fool than you were with Will Parker.*

She took a deep breath and stood up. "Be there in a sec," she called back.

With no thoughts of Nick Garroway as her person, she told herself.

How she'd accomplish that when she was going to a family dinner of his was beyond her, but one thing at a time, right?

According to Nick, his dad and her prospective client were both thrilled about the idea of babies coming to their family dinner tonight. That gave Brooke a good feeling about Jeb Garroway. Anyone who'd welcome the wedding planner's twin babies to a dinner gathering had to be all right. By her anyway.

"What did he say when you told him your temporary job was as a nanny—and for the wedding planner?" she asked as they pulled into the driveway of his father's house.

Nick turned off the engine. "He said, 'You always do your own thing, that's for sure.'" I couldn't tell if he meant that in good way or a bad way."

Brooke got out and opened the back door to take out

Morgan's car seat. "I think most people admire those who do their own thing. Even when it doesn't serve them."

"I don't know about that," Nick said, unlatching Mikey's seat and carrying him in one hand while he grabbed the gift bag containing the bottle of champagne he'd stopped for. "Most people I know want their loved ones to toe the line. Do what's expected of them."

"Welcome!" came a male voice from the doorway as an adorable brown-and-white cocker spaniel came padding out, wagging its tail.

Brooke turned to see a man in his late fifties, tall like Nick, but with lighter hair and softer features, and a woman heading toward them.

"I'm Jeb Garroway, Nick's father. And this lovely woman is my fiancée, Cathy Wylie. The floppy-eared guy is Fritz."

"So nice to meet you," Brooke said. "And hello, very cute Fritz."

The dog sniffed her leg and padded back inside.

"Such a small world," Cathy said, smiling at them. "To have my fiancé's son working as the nanny for the wedding planner I made an appointment with. Something here has definitely been charted in the stars." Like Jeb, Cathy was in her late fifties. She had wavy blond hair to her shoulders and sparkling green eyes.

"I believe the correct word is *manny*," came another voice from the doorway.

Brooke glanced up. A guy who looked something like Nick stood there, holding a drink. He was tall and muscular and good-looking, but his half-wary, half-scowling expression took something away. The infamous brother, she presumed.

"Meet Brandon, my other son," Jeb said. "Jeb, this is Brooke Timber."

Brandon nodded at her, and she smiled back.

"And who are these darlings?" Cathy asked, peering into the car seats. "Let's get them inside and you can introduce us."

They headed in, with Brooke aware of the tension between Nick and his brother. Everyone seemed aware of it but was ignoring it for the time being.

They went into a big living room that had a gorgeous stone fireplace with two sofas set around it. Fritz curled up on a red dog bed by the fireplace. Brooke set the baby seats on the rug beside the huge wood coffee table, and Cathy rushed over to coo at them.

"This is Morgan and this is Mikey. They're three months old," Brooke said.

Cathy touched a hand to her chest. "They're precious."

"They are, indeed," Jeb said.

From the way Cathy slid her hand into Jeb's and squeezed, Brooke could tell that Jeb was thinking of his own two boys when they'd been babies. And that Cathy had had a hand in helping Jeb accept his older son for who he was, not who Jeb had wanted him to be. Or become.

Brooke smiled at Jeb and Cathy. "And luckily it's close to their bedtime, so they should conk out any minute. We'll have a nice, peaceful dinner and can talk all about the dream wedding you envision."

"Of course, if one or both get fussy, you've got your nanny right here to step in," Cathy said with a grin. "I love it. Former soldier turned baby whisperer."

Brandon rolled his eyes. "That's not a thing."

"Well, it is now," Jeb said with a piercing look at his younger son.

Brooke glanced at Nick, who was sitting as far away from his brother as possible while still being in the same room.

"A *temporary* thing, though," Brandon remarked. "Isn't that what you said, Nick?"

Nick nodded. "I'm at Brooke's service until her regular nanny returns at the start of August."

"So, then you'll come work at Garroway Paper, right?" Brandon asked, staring at Nick. "I'll have to train you, but we'll start you in sales and you'll pick it up fast. I'm sure you'll be regional manager by Christmas. Our guy right now is just about ready for a promotion. Then in a year, we can talk a VP title."

Nick cleared his throat. "We're here to talk dad and Cathy's wedding." He turned to Cathy. "Brooke said something about a wellness retreat?"

Brooke glanced at Brandon. The guy was frowning at being shut down, but at least he wasn't insisting on an answer.

"Sagebrush Sanctuary and Retreat," Cathy said. "It's just an hour from here but pure rural. The cabins blend right into the surrounding nature. It's so peaceful. The center offers yoga retreats, mindful-living seminars, everything to do with a calm mind and healthful body. I'd love to have the ceremony outside, in the gazebo, and the reception in one of the open-air structures."

"Sounds lovely," Brooke said. "I did some research on the place, so we can talk about options tonight."

Cathy smiled. "Great." She stood. "Let's head into the dining room. Dinner is ready."

Nick picked up both baby carriers and followed Cathy, with Brooke beside him. Jeb and Brandon were behind them.

"Have to say, I never thought I'd see Nick holding a baby, let alone two," Brandon quipped. "Wonders never cease, I suppose. Gives me hope that he'll take his rightful place with us at Garroway Paper."

Brooke turned just in time to see Brandon lay a hand on Nick's back, and she could see Nick stiffen.

"Ga ba da!" Mikey said, waving his arms. "Ba da!"

Nick seemed glad for Mikey's interruption as they entered the large dining room. "If none of you speak baby, that means 'pick me up right now!'"

"Oh, I speak baby," Jeb said. "You two were champion babblers."

Brandon laughed. "I never babbled."

"You most certainly did," Jeb said. "And I always knew what you were trying to say."

"Come on, you weren't exactly a hands-on father, even when we were talking in full sentences," Nick said, and then froze the moment the words were out of his mouth.

Brooke knew he regretted it, that it had just tumbled out before he could think, before he could stop himself.

Jeb stiffened too, his expression tightening. "No, I wasn't. But when my boys have children, I'll certainly be a hands-on grandfather."

"We can only move forward, not backward," Cathy said, nodding. "Nick, you can set the carriers down on the floor." She pointed to the left.

Nick closed his eyes for a second, then opened them, moving near a window. "Dad, I'm sorry. I didn't mean—"

"You'll say anything to defend betraying the family," Brandon snapped. "As if Dad working all the time had anything to do with you leaving."

Now the entire room was full of stiff, unsmiling people. Except for the babies, who were both wiggling and wanted to be out of their carriers.

Nick's expression was grim as he took out Mikey, and Brooke rushed over to take Morgan. They stood in front of the window, the filmy gauze curtains filtering the early evening light. Nick had told Brooke he'd changed and fed both boys before they'd left, so the babies should require just a little soothing and swaying, and they'd be ready to be put back in their carriers and down for the next few hours.

"Hush, little baby," Nick whisper-sang, rocking Mikey gently back and forth.

It amazed Brooke how Nick was able to compartmentalize. His focus was laser sharp on the baby in arms. Not the tension in the room. Or what he'd said.

"As I live and breathe," Brandon muttered, shaking his head. "All you need is the Mary Poppins umbrella."

Nick let out a ragged sigh. "I'd ask you what your problem is, Brandon, but I know what it is. Let's leave our issues out of tonight. This is about Dad and Cathy and their wedding."

So much for the laser-focus, Brooke thought, her stomach sinking.

"So big of you," Brandon said, but yanked out his chair and sat down.

Jeb sent each of his boys a sharp look and sat down, as well.

"Well, this guy is ready for bed," Nick said. "How about his twin?" he asked Brooke.

Brooke forced a smile. "Yup, he's ready."

They put the babies back in the carriers on the floor. Between the dim lighting, the candles on the table and the curtains filtering the still-strong sunshine at past six o'clock, this setting and hum of voices was ideal for baby sleep. Both little ones fought their eyes closing, but with a few rocks of the carriers, Mikey and Morgan were asleep.

"Ah, success," Nick said as he moved to the table and held out a chair for Brooke—the one directly across from his brother, so that he wouldn't have to sit there. Then he sat beside Brooke. Hey, she got it. She wouldn't want to face that scowl for the next hour either if it were directed at her.

"Brandon, will you help me bring everything out?" Cathy asked.

Brandon leaped up. "Sure." He followed Cathy into the kitchen, and there was some murmuring, which Brooke assumed was Cathy asking Brandon to chill out for the sake of their dad.

Moments later they returned with a huge tossed salad, an amazing-looking pasta dish and bruschetta.

"Help yourselves to whatever appeals," Cathy said, and they all stood and heaped their plates full. "Brooke, did you always want to be a wedding planner?" Cathy asked as they sat down, ready to eat.

Brooke nodded. "I think I got lucky—being a wedding planner was all I've wanted to do since I was very young. My grandmother started the business and I was her apprentice for as long as I can remember. Brides seemed like princesses to me, royalty for the day. I loved the idea of planning something so special. Wedding planner feels like an honor to me."

"I'm glad you see it that way," Cathy said. "Because *special* is the word for the wedding I envision."

Brooke smiled, heaping some pasta and salad on her plate. She had a feeling she and Cathy would get along just fine.

"That's the way I've always looked at family businesses," Brandon said, then took a bite of the pasta. "You apprentice young, learn the ropes and then suddenly you're running the enterprise. I'm impressed, Brooke."

She slid an uneasy glance at Nick, who was staring at his plate. "Well, as I said, I loved the world of weddings. It's what I wanted to do with my life. But what if I wanted to be a chef or an ambassador in the foreign service or a teacher? I think my grandmother would have wanted me to follow my passion."

Brandon sipped his wine. "She might have said so, but I'm sure it would have broken her heart to have you ignore the family business that put a roof over your head and food on the table."

"Oh, Brandon, give it a rest," Nick said. "We all get it. I did something different with my life and you didn't like it."

"No one liked it," Brandon snarled.

Nick slugged down his sparkling water. Brooke and Cathy made tight smiles at each other. And Jeb Garroway just looked uncomfortable.

"Why don't we talk privately after dinner," Nick said to his brother. "For now let's enjoy this delicious meal. The pasta is amazing, Cathy."

Cathy beamed. "Your dad made the pasta. I did the bruschetta and the salad."

"Wow, Dad," Nick said. "I didn't know you started cooking. That's great."

His dad smiled, the tension between the two of them thankfully forgotten. "And hopefully you'll come over often so I can try out my mad skills on you. I'm taking an Italian-cooking course at the community center."

Brooke grinned. Based on everything Nick had told her about his dad, it sure sounded like Cathy had had an amazingly positive influence on him.

Nick's shoulders visibly relaxed. His dad's acceptance of him and warm welcome meant the world to him, clearly.

But soon enough the pasta was gone and only crumbs of the bruschetta remained.

"Let's go into dad's office," Nick said to his brother.

Hopefully they'd talk and come out with their arms around each other, each accepting the other's differences.

Brooke, Cathy and Jeb watched the two Garroways head out of the dining room. A door closed.

"Well, fingers crossed," Jeb said. "I've talked to Brandon until I had no words left, and he was stubborn as ever about how Nick 'betrayed' us. I tried to tell him that we looked at that all wrong, that we should be proud of who he was, who he is, but he's just stuck on it."

Brooke heard voices coming from the room the brothers had gone into. Raised voices.

"Oh, so now you're Mr. Family Oriented?" Brandon's raised voice said. "Giving a crap about Dad? Please."

Uh oh. Brooke hadn't heard what Nick had said that had gotten that response.

"You have some damned nerve, Nick," Brandon continued, his voice booming. "First you disappear on us for ten years—eleven years—to do what you want, and now that you're back, what do you do? Get a job working for someone else. And as a *nanny*? Where is your shame?"

"My shame?" Nick repeated, his own voice not quite as loud but stone cold. "About being a nanny? Are you serious?"

"Oh, wait, I mean *manny*." Brandon laughed. "Do you want to guess how many people stopped me today on Main Street to tell me my brother, the soldier, is a manny? I told the first two that they were mistaken. By the fourth time I realized it had to be true. A manny," he repeated with a dry chuckle.

Brooke, Jeb and Cathy all glanced uncomfortably at one another, then looked away.

"They got along so well when they were kids," Jeb whispered, shaking his head. "I hate that this is how things are. Nick was right—I wasn't around much when they were young because I put work first. And when things turned ugly between them, I threw myself even more into work because I couldn't deal with it." He let out a breath and stared down at the table.

"Hey," Cathy said, putting an arm around him. "I think a family wedding will help bring them together. Bring you all together."

Brooke sure hoped so.

"We're done here," Nick said—through gritted teeth, if Brooke wasn't mistaken.

"Why the hell would you waste your time as a baby-sitter?" Brandon asked as a door opened and footsteps pounded toward the dining room. Nick entered the room, his expression furious, his brother trailing him. "Just tell me that. Tell us *all* that."

Nick ignored him and walked over to the baby seats on the floor, where Mikey was beginning to fuss a bit. Nick unlatched the harness and picked up the baby, cuddling him close against his chest. "I've got you," he said softly to Mikey, swaying him in his arms a bit.

Brooke glanced at Brandon, who looked half incredulous, half disgusted. It couldn't be fun to be that disgruntled, she thought, and she had a feeling Brandon Garroway was disgruntled all of the time.

"I worked hard on the tiramisu for dessert, so you two will sit here and enjoy it and be civil," Jeb said, pointing a finger at his sons.

Neither Garroway son responded.

"I'll help bring out dessert," Brooke said, following Cathy into the kitchen.

"A change of subject is definitely in order," Cathy whispered in the kitchen. "Let's talk wedding. That should shut up the guys."

Brooke laughed. She knew she liked Cathy.

They brought in the tiramisu, laughing over Jeb's account of failing miserably the first time, messing up the steps his cooking teacher had listed on the recipe. The dessert was definitely missing something—had he forgotten to soak the ladyfingers in coffee?—but was still scrumptious.

Jeb turned the conversation to Brooke, asking about the wedding-planning business and the craziest wedding she'd ever planned.

"The one where both the bride and groom got cold feet, right before the ceremony was to start," Brooke said, shaking her head as she remembered. "Big wedding, over 250 guests. But it turned out the best man, the groom's brother, had been madly in love with his lifelong best friend, the bride's sister, and he proposed right there, and the wedding turned into an engagement party. Both families were there, so it worked out."

"That is crazy," Jeb said, shaking his head.

"I had the big wedding the first time around," Cathy said. "Now my dream wedding is a small, intimate affair with a view of the mountains. Just close family and good friends. My two daughters—they're nineteen and twenty-one—will be my maids of honor, so that's it for the bridal party."

"And I'd like the two of you to be my best men," Jeb said, looking from Brandon to Nick.

Brooke slid a glance at the Garroway brothers. They both looked miserable under their tight smiles.

"Of course, Dad," Brandon said. "You can always count on *me*."

Nick smiled at his father. "Thank you for asking. It'd be my honor."

Brooke caught Nick's brother rolling his eyes.

Ooh boy, the wedding preparations were not going to be fun where these two were concerned.

For the next ten minutes, Brooke and Cathy talked

about the venue, food and flowers. Cathy was a vegan and didn't drink alcohol, and the wedding would not be typical. No problem. Brooke knew three vegan caterers whose food was amazing.

"There's one small thing, though," Cathy said. "Well, a big thing. My friend who owns the retreat center needs to up the date to *next* weekend. The whole weekend will be ours, but it's certainly short notice for you, Brooke."

"Next weekend?" Brandon sputtered. "What about our business trip to see the Midwest and Southern regional sales managers?"

"That's what right-hand employees are for," Jeb said. "Between our VPs, the trip will go fine without us. And besides, you could use a weekend away."

"I wouldn't call a 'wellness center' a vacation," Brandon muttered under his breath. "Do people chant there?"

Cathy laughed. "Only if they want. It's about nature and relaxing, Brandon. You'll love it there. I promise."

"I'll drive out to the center tomorrow, see if I can meet with the events manager, and then plan out the entire wedding, talk to my vendors and give you the details by tomorrow night. Sound good?"

"Perfect," Cathy said. "I leave my wedding in your capable hands."

Yes! Client secured!

Good news for Brooke, indeed. But how the two Garroway brothers would spend a weekend together—a dry weekend, at that—at a wellness center, without pushing each other off a mountain cliff, was something else entirely.

Chapter Seven

"What I want to know is, do any families actually get along all the time?" Nick asked as he carried both sleeping babies in their car seats into Brooke's house. "Where everyone respects everyone else's choices and everyone is just happy to be together? Does such a thing exist?"

She locked the door behind him and followed him up the stairs, with the cats trailing them. It was the first thing he'd said beyond the smallest of small talk on the way home from his dad's house about the weather and the light traffic and the lack of humidity.

She hadn't hit him with questions in the car, though she had a ton. She was dying to talk to him about the wedding, how he felt about standing up for his dad, what it meant to him, though she'd been able to tell he'd been deeply touched. She'd had the sense that Nick needed to be alone with his thoughts, so she'd kept the conversation to the mundane.

Snowball and Smudge disappeared into Nick's room. They liked to sleep on his bed, even though they'd never spent much time in the guest room. Baby whisperer and cat conqueror. Amazing.

In the nursery they each took a sleeping baby, very carefully transferring the twins to their cribs, and though Mikey stirred, neither woke up.

They tiptoed out and Brooke hoped Nick wouldn't go into his room and shut the door—shut her *out*. She wanted to talk, wanted to answer his questions. But she wasn't sure if he'd meant it rhetorically or not.

Her heart gave a little leap when he walked past his room and headed downstairs.

"Beer?" he asked, walking into the kitchen.

"I'd love one," she said, and he took two out of the fridge and went into the living room, sinking down on the sofa. She sat beside him, taking the bottle and twisting off the cap. "To be honest, I don't know how families are. It was always just me and my grandmother, since my parents died when I was so young. She was always supportive of me, and I was a pretty easy kid and teenager, I'd say. Didn't get in trouble, got good grades, dated nice boys."

"Wanted to follow in her footsteps in the family business," he added, taking a swig of his beer.

"I'm sure that it made it easy for both of us, the shared love of all things weddings. But paper is another story, I guess. Although I once watched a documentary about how paper is made, and I was riveted."

He burst out laughing. "Oh, wait, you're serious." He

gave her shoulder a playful squeeze and she wished he'd pull her into his arms. They were so close on the sofa, with only a few inches separating their arms and thighs. "That would earn you major points with the Garroways."

She took a sip of her beer to refocus from her wayward thoughts. "You know, now that I think about it, I had friends with all kinds of families—the TV kind and the big-problem kind. But no one I know really lived a charmed life. Stuff happens."

"That's very true," he said. "Though for a while there, I had it very good." He leaned his head back against the sofa. "I wish I hadn't let Brandon get to me tonight. I walked into that dinner with my back up, and because of that, I said stuff I shouldn't have to my dad when he's done a total 360. I have to stop being ready for combat."

She touched his arm, then quickly removed it. "Brandon's a tough one—I'll give you that. Your dad said you and your brother were very close when you were kids?"

"Very close," he said, with his arms crossed over his chest. "Especially when our mom first got sick, and our dad was always working, even when he was home, Brandon came to me a lot for his questions and when he had problems. I'd spend hours teaching myself math concepts he was struggling with so I could help with homework and to study for tests. For a couple of the hard tween years, he had issues with friends, and so I'd hang with him on weekends, take him fishing or to the movies and then Five Guys. We'd talk about everything and nothing. He had a lot of anxiety about our mom being sick and not wanting to bother her."

He stopped talking and looked up at the ceiling.

"I'm so sorry about your mother."

He nodded. "Me too. She was a wonderful person. It kills me to think I disappointed her, you know? Especially when she was so weak and tired from chemo. But she never said anything about my joining Garroway Paper. I always took that to mean she liked that I was going my own way."

"Did she say anything about that at all?"

"She just said what she always said, that I marched to my own drum, and would pat my hand. I thought that was her way of approving of me." His voice got heavy with emotion and he looked to the right, away from Brooke. "But she and Brandon were always very close, much closer than I was with her or my dad. When he said I broke her heart, I believed him. I cursed myself for being so selfish, for not making her final time more comfortable by knowing her eldest was joining the family business, that I was settled where I should be."

"But it wasn't where you should have been, Nick," Brooke said, this time daring to reach for his hand and holding on to it for a moment. "And it sounds like your mother knew that and respected it."

He gave something of a shrug and she let go of his hand. "Well, all that was a long time ago. I hate disappointing people, but I've done a lot of that during the past eleven years. So it's a good thing that I'm here for just a short time. If I let down you or those twins, I'd…"

He got up and walked over to the sliding glass doors to the patio, looking out at the night.

She walked up to him and risked putting her hands on his shoulders. He stiffened at the touch but he didn't move away. "You're a dream, Nick Garroway. You're heaven-sent. You couldn't possibly disappoint us."

He turned around, his blue eyes intense on her. "I won't intend to. But that's not what matters in the end."

"Nick, circumstances are circumstances. You can't control everything. Or anything, really."

"I think I hear one of the twins," he said, but she knew neither had made a peep. The conversation had gone places she hadn't expected, and it got to be too much for him. He headed for the stairs.

"I know exactly why you're here," she called after him.

He stopped in his tracks but didn't turn around.

"You made a promise to check on me, to see that I was all right. I wasn't, so you're here. How could you possibly disappoint me or the twins when your entire point is to take care of us until my regular nanny returns?"

Jeez. Obtuse much, Brooke? She knew damned well how. By *leaving*.

He did turn around then and looked at her. "Because things always get complicated. Don't they."

He went upstairs and this time she didn't expect him to come back down.

He was right. Things always did get complicated. Exhibit A was the fact that she was falling in love with him.

Last night, when Brooke had walked up behind him and put her hands on his shoulders, he'd almost turned and wrapped his own arms around her. He'd needed the hug after that dinner from hell. Well, not all of it had been hellish. It had felt so good to be there, sitting at the table with his family again. Not only invited to his dad's wedding but to be a *part* of it.

He'd been overwhelmed by it all, and then the conversation with Brooke had poked places inside him.

But he was glad he'd controlled himself and hadn't reached for her. She'd once smartly put a stop to something happening between them, and if she hadn't last night, adding sex, or even just kissing, to what was between them would bring those complications crashing down on his head.

He was glad she'd brought up the reason he was here—because of the promise. Giving into his attraction for her, knowing that he couldn't be what she needed or wanted in the long run, meant having to control himself for the short term. No matter how hard it was. He'd tossed and turned for so long last night, wanting to go next door and slip into bed beside her, forget everything but how good she'd feel in his arms.

But he'd known the next morning, he'd just have to add "last night" to the list of complications, so he'd stayed put.

And then an unexpected text from his brother around midnight had done a great job of taking his mind off Brooke.

Last night got out of hand. Sorry. Come by the office tomorrow at 5:00 p.m., if you can. We're having a small celebration for the company's fortieth year in business. It's a surprise—but I know Dad would love to see you there.
—B

This morning, Nick still couldn't decide if his brother was truly extending the ole olive branch or being manipulative. But an apology was something, especially for Brandon, and a celebration for forty years in business was a big deal. Of course Nick would go.

He forced himself to wait until 8:59 a.m. to go downstairs, not wanting to take time away from Brooke with her boys. She was in the kitchen, pouring a cup of coffee as the twins stared at the gently spinning mobiles attached to their swings.

"One for you too?" she asked him.

He nodded. "I'll need caffeine today. My brother asked me to go to a surprise fortieth celebration for Garroway Paper at the office today."

"That must mean you're going," she said. "Good first step for both of you."

"Both of us? Meaning?"

"Meaning you're both trying. He extended an invitation and you're accepting. That's how it works."

Nick nodded and already wanted to talk about something—anything—else. He added cream and sugar to his coffee, took a big gulp, and then turned his attention to the Timber twins. "How are my favorite babies, today?"

"Ba ga!" Mikey said.

"Ga!" Morgan added, tossing his stuffed donkey on the floor with a laugh.

"You little imp," Nick said, giving each boy a kiss on the head. "So, you two, how about a walk through town and then lunch in the park. You can visit your favorite squirrels."

"Sounds like a plan," Brooke said. "Especially because I have *a lot* of work to do. I'll be driving up to the wellness venue to get going on your dad and Cathy's wedding, and then I'll be making a thousand calls about

"4 for 4" MINI-SURVEY

We are prepared to **REWARD** you with 2 FREE books and 2 FREE gifts for completing our MINI SURVEY!

FREE Value Over **$20!**

You'll get...

TWO FREE BOOKS & TWO FREE GIFTS

just for participating in our Mini Survey

Dear Reader,

IT'S A FACT: if you answer 4 quick questions, we'll send you **4 FREE REWARDS!**

I'm not kidding you. As a leading publisher of women's fiction, we value your opinions... and your time. That's why we are prepared to **reward** you handsomely for completing our mini-survey. In fact, we have 4 Free Rewards for you, including 2 free books and 2 free gifts.

As you may have guessed, that's why our mini-survey is called **"4 for 4".** Answer 4 questions and get 4 Free Rewards. It's that simple!

Thank you for participating in our survey,

Pam Powers

To get your 4 FREE REWARDS:
Complete the survey below and return the insert today to receive 2 FREE BOOKS and 2 FREE GIFTS guaranteed!

"4 for 4" MINI-SURVEY

1 Is reading one of your favorite hobbies?
☐ YES   ☐ NO

2 Do you prefer to read instead of watch TV?
☐ YES   ☐ NO

3 Do you read newspapers and magazines?
☐ YES   ☐ NO

4 Do you enjoy trying new book series with FREE BOOKS?
☐ YES   ☐ NO

YES! I have completed the above Mini-Survey. Please send me my 4 FREE REWARDS (worth over $20 retail). I understand that I am under no obligation to buy anything, as explained on the back of this card.

235/335 HDL GNU7

FIRST NAME	LAST NAME

ADDRESS

APT.#	CITY

STATE/PROV.	ZIP/POSTAL CODE

◄ If offer card is missing write to: Reader Service, P.O. Box 1341, Buffalo, NY 14240-8531 or visit www.ReaderService.com ◄

BUSINESS REPLY MAIL
FIRST-CLASS MAIL   PERMIT NO. 717   BUFFALO, NY

POSTAGE WILL BE PAID BY ADDRESSEE

READER SERVICE
PO BOX 1341
BUFFALO NY 14240-8571

NO POSTAGE
NECESSARY
IF MAILED
IN THE
UNITED STATES

the Satler triplets' wedding, because guess who hired me, after all?"

Without thinking, Nick took Brooke's hand and pulled her up for a celebratory hug, wrapping his arms tightly around her. She hugged him tightly too and he never wanted to let go. "Congratulations," he said against her hair, which smelled like flowers and sunscreen lotion.

"If you hadn't walked in when you did, I can't even imagine. No Satler wedding. No nanny. I'd be worrying right now about everything. Instead I feel like everything is possible."

"Good." He pulled back, instantly missing the feel of her against him. "Go work. I've got these little rug rats."

She grinned and gave each boy a kiss on the head, then left the room. He heard her footsteps go into the Dream Weddings office and the door shut.

He could still feel her in his arms.

He got out of the house in record time, needing air and space, and to get Brooke out of his head. In a ten minute walk down Main Street, pushing the stroller and minding his own business, he got four "so, you're the manny I heard about" and two eavesdropped "I'll bet they're involved." And since a group of smiling women with yoga mats were approaching and looked like they were about to pounce on him, he swerved the stroller left, down a side street that led to the three schools in town.

"That's where your mommy and your manny went to elementary school," he told Morgan and Mikey, stopping by the fenced playground. "Different times, since I'm five years older. I hope she didn't have mean Mrs.

Buckworth as a substitute." He'd lived for the yard in those days, waiting for the recess dismissal so he could rush out to the tire swings and slides, and leap across the monkey bars. "And this is where you'll go. Your very first day of school will be right here."

He glanced up at the one-story, winding building. Brooke had grown up in Wedlock Creek, and he was pretty sure her parents had too, since she lived in her grandmother's house. Generations of Timbers had put down roots in Wedlock Creek. Sometimes that seemed like a good thing, roots and family.

But his family tree felt all twisted, even with his father's warm welcome and the upcoming wedding this weekend.

Nick spent the next hour wheeling the stroller all over the three campuses, pointing out his middle school and high school. Then he headed back to Main Street and to the library to take out a few new picture books.

As he pointed out all the places he knew, buildings and shops and the movie theater where he'd seen favorite films with his family as a teen, no feelings of familial pride overtook him. No thoughts of roots and family bonds. He could barely stomach the idea of walking into Garroway Paper, because of what it represented to him—the big issue between him and his family.

As he passed Wedlock Creek Gifts, he stopped in for a wedding card, grateful the wedding section wasn't an entire aisle like the birthday section. He liked the fronts of some, but the inside messages were too hokey. A bunch poured it on way too thick. Then others didn't say enough. *Congratulations* wouldn't quite cut it.

"Which one, guys?" he asked the twins, who were looking at the bright cards.

"Ba!" Mikey said and laughed.

"Ga ba!" Morgan added, flinging his little stuffed monkey at the bottom row of cards.

As Nick picked up the monkey, his gaze landed on a card with a die-cut bride and groom underlaid with velum. His father would appreciate the papery aspects, for sure. Inside, the greeting read, "All my best wishes for a lifetime of happiness. You deserve it."

Huh. That was it. That was exactly how Nick felt about his father's second marriage.

"Thanks, Morgan," he said to the baby, giving his head a little rub. "You've got great taste."

Once outside, he sat down on the bench and grabbed a pen from the stroller bag, going with the moment to write something in the card while he was in the mindset. Otherwise he'd scrawl *congrats* underneath and sign his name, and he wanted to write what was in his head.

His heart. Which was still beating, after all.

He found himself filling the entire left side of the card. How glad he was to be back in his dad's life. How happy he was that the couple had found each other, and that he looked forward to sharing in their life together.

Before he could tell himself he'd gone overboard and had gotten all mushy, he sealed the envelope and slipped it in the stroller bag.

"Sometimes I surprise myself, guys," he told the twins as he stood and started wheeling toward Oak Lane.

When Nick came downstairs at 4:45 p.m., in a dark gray suit and shiny black shoes, Brooke did a double take and then couldn't stop staring. She knew why too. Yes, he looked very handsome. But it was much more than that.

He looked like a groom.

Granted, the suit wasn't a tux and Nick had forgone a tie, but Brooke had seen a zillion grooms in her years as a wedding planner, and her first thought at seeing Nick come down those stairs was *husband-to-be*. And a mighty good-looking one, at that.

"Wow," she said, putting Mikey into his swing, beside Morgan on the table. "You clean up well."

He smiled that dazzler that always also stopped her in her tracks. "I thought I'd blend in better in this thing than standing out in a T-shirt and jeans as 'the son who didn't join the family business.'"

"Looking forward to it at all?" she asked. "Or all dread?"

"I'm glad to be there for my dad. And to be part of something special to him. Forty years in business is a big deal. But yeah, there's the dread part. I have a feeling my brother is going to try to sell me on the company, lay on the guilt, that it's time, that I did my thing and now it's time to do the family thing."

"Why is it so important to him?" she asked. "That's what I can't figure out."

"Good question. I've thought about that a lot over the years. Maybe because he always saw it as his path, and since he once looked up to me as the older brother, he'd assumed it was my plan too and I blindsided him? I'm not sure. He really does look at it as a betrayal."

"I'll say it a million times, Nick. No one's life should be dictated by someone else's choices or dreams. Your brother was happy to step into his father's shoes and follow his footsteps. You weren't. Nothing about that makes your brother a better person than you or right."

"But I did break my mother's heart," he said. "I have to live with that. Choices we make affect other people. No way around that. No matter how right or wrong we are. People get hurt."

Didn't she know it. "I don't want to say something so trite like 'but that's life,' but Nick, it is. People do get hurt. Yes. I got hurt when Will Parker acted like our time together was nothing. And when my pregnancy meant absolutely less than nothing to him. But life goes on. Was I supposed to stay in bed, under the covers, for months, even though I wanted to?"

"Are you saying that's what I'm doing?" He stiffened, as though he hadn't meant to say that out loud.

He was *half* under the covers, half not—but because he had to be, not because he wanted to be. "I think you're trying. You're going to the party. You could have made an excuse. But you want to join in the celebration, mostly because it's important to your father and brother. That's big."

"How did we go from 'you clean up nice' to this conversation?" he asked.

"Neither of us are much for small talk. Way I see it, you might as well say what's really on your mind and what's really the issue. Or what's the point?"

He smiled. "I've always preferred to ignore and deflect."

"Sorry, house rules."

He laughed and the sound was like music and magic to her ears. She wanted to rush into his arms and hug him, tell him he was a good person, the best person she knew, and that everything would be okay. But honestly she had no idea if that were true. Which parts and how okay any of it would be.

Including her heart, which was at serious risk of getting broken again.

Chapter Eight

Garroway Paper was in a very dull five-story office building, in a small industrial park en route to the freeway out of Wedlock Creek. The company had the entire third floor, and the seventeen employees were in the large conference room. Nick glanced at the Garroway Paper logo on the wall above the long credenza. Once, he'd looked at that logo with pride. When he was a kid, he thought his father was like a king or the president of the United States for having his name on a company, and he had to admit that the logo still spoke to that little kid somewhere inside him. His family was important to him, so he wasn't all that surprised.

He shook a lot of hands as Brandon introduced him to sales reps, the controller, administrative assistants, vendors and the marketing manager—who'd immediately asked if she could do a social-media blast about a Garroway son returning home from a long military career. Brandon approved it with gusto before Nick could say a word. He shrugged it off, but he didn't like his military career being a bonus only when it looked good for the company. Whatever. He was long used to the machine.

With his brother chatting away to a vendor, Nick moved into a corner next to the buffet table and helped himself to something that looked like a very small quiche. He glanced around the room for his dad and found him surrounded by an animated group. His father sure looked happy. Jeb was in his element here. The smile, much like he'd had at the dinner where Nick had met Cathy, satisfied something inside Nick. His dad was happy here. Brandon was happy here. And Nick was happy for them. *I'm glad I came*, he thought.

"I can tell you feel like you're missing out," Brandon said, appearing on his left. His brother put an arm around his shoulder that suddenly felt like a clamp. "Your expression gives you away. You want a piece of this. And you can have it with a simple yes. There's even a private office waiting for you. Did you know that Dad kept it open for you all these years?"

Nick had gone from anger at Brandon's manipulative mumbo jumbo to the mini quiche in his stomach turning to sludge. His father had kept an office open for Nick? What?

"Come on, I'll show you," Brandon said, and Nick had no intention of following his brother out the door and to the office, but he had to get the hell out of this room, which was suddenly closing in on him. He could make one sharp right and disappear into the stairwell, gulp in some air. "Here it is," Brandon said, gesturing at an ajar office door, the neon-red Stairwell sign so close—yet so far.

At least his name wasn't on a placard on the door. Brandon stepped into the medium-sized room. Desk, chair, lamp, phone. Credenza. Small bookcase. Window facing the parking lot.

"Of course, if you prefer a view of the gardens out front, we can switch someone for you," Brandon said. "I'm thinking two weeks of intensive training by me and all of the department heads—of course, most departments are one-person operations, so we'll have to look at their schedules—and within a couple of months, you'll be regional manager. Like I said before, by Christmas I don't see why see why you couldn't be VP of operations. And sorry, older bro, but I'll always be President, so you'll have to settle for second in line to me. Seniority over age. You get it, right?"

Oh, he got it. This invitation was a ploy, just as Nick had suspected. Not about having him share in something special to his dad and to the company, but trying to force him into this office—where he didn't belong. Where he'd never belong.

"Brandon, I'm here today to celebrate the company's fortieth. That's all."

His brother scowled. "Right. I forgot. Being a nanny—a *manny*," he added, with extra scorn in his head shake, "is your chosen career path, now that you're a civilian."

"I told you, the nanny job is temporary."

Brandon's eyes lit up. "Ah, so it's just a summer

thing? So, when shall we expect you? How about the Tuesday after Labor Day? Fitting, don't you think?"

Long, hard sigh. "I'm not planning to join Garroway Paper, Brandon."

"What the hell are you planning?"

"I'm going to buy a ranch, a couple thousand acres. Cattle, sheep, chickens."

His brother stared at him. "What the ever-loving hell? Now you're a cowboy?"

"That's the goal," he said. "I've been thinking about it a long time. Remember when we'd visit Aunt Ginny on the ranch? It sparked something in me back then."

That small farm really had. The Garroways had driven the two hours out, and the minute Nick had gotten out of the car, breathed in that country air mingled with the scent of hay and horses, he'd felt the strangest sensation that he'd realized was akin to homecoming. It was the same feeling he got every time he came back stateside after a tour. Because he hadn't been welcome in his family home, Nick had stayed at guest ranches in Wyoming, researching the idea of having his own place one day. The more he read up, the more he visited, the more he talked to ranchers and cowboys, the more he knew it was the life he wanted.

Nick scowled. "Aunt Ginny was a crazy recluse who had two horses and four goats and operated a small goat-milk business, which she put her own labels on and sold in local stores. That's not ranching."

"It was to her," Nick pointed out. Aunt Ginny had passed away years ago. She was their mother's sister and had never married. She'd always said she wanted to live life her way, on her terms, on her own land, and have animals for company instead of people. Nick had always admired her. But to the family, she'd been crazy Aunt Ginny, even to Nick's mom, who often claimed not to understand her sister.

"Why start something when something already exists?" Brandon asked. "That's what I don't get. Garroway Paper is here and waiting for you. We need you, Nick."

Stab to the heart. Brandon had said that before, a few times, and it had always deflated him, whooshed the anger right out. And made him feel guilty as hell. *We need you.*

"Brandon, time to cut the cake!" a woman called out.

Nick glanced toward the voice. Saved.

"We'll continue this conversation," Brandon said, then walked back into the conference room.

Not if I can help it, Nick thought, the collar of his shirt tightening on him as he headed back too, staying near the door—the exit.

A huge five-layer cake that read Congrats, Garroway Paper: 40 Years! in red icing was brought to the long table. Jeb made the first slice of the cake to cheers and clapping, Brandon wolf whistling beside their dad.

As Nick clapped too, he caught his father's eye. The warm nod Jeb gave him touched something inside Nick, filled some hole that been there a long time. *Okay, I needed that*, he thought, feeling glad he'd come.

But the gleam in his brother's eye poked at his gut. As plates of cake made their way around the room, Nick slipped out and went down that stairwell and into the air, sucking in a long, hard breath.

What a day, Brooke thought, plunking down on the sofa, with one eye on the twins as they gnawed their little chew toys in their swings, and her mind going over details of the Garroway-Wylie wedding. Every detail was in place for this Saturday's big event. She'd spent the morning at the Sagebrush Sanctuary and Retreat and had managed to book the caterer, florist, jazz band and minister, while sipping a fruit-infused water, on a floor cushion in the gazebo where Jeb and Cathy would have their ceremony. Brooke had just followed up via text with the events manager, and everything on her list had been crossed off with a thrilling *done*.

She liked being so busy. Today her mind had been on her job and not her love life. Even if her job was a celebration of love itself. Oy.

Brooke loved that Cathy would wear the dress her mother had worn to travel to her honeymoon sixty years ago, and her daughters would each wear floaty satin sand-colored dresses they'd fallen in love with in a boutique last weekend, during a whirlwind shopping trip. The Garroway men would each wear a sand-colored suit that Jeb had arranged for at a fancy men's store, and go tieless in keeping with the outdoor, yoga-esque theme.

With all of that settled, she did a little work on the Satler wedding, organizing the emails each triplet had sent about what was a must for "their day" and what they could compromise on in the name of sisterhood. Shelley had insisted on each sister having her own cake, but Samantha had thought that would be weird at cake-cutting time, since none of the guests would want to miss the first cutting of the cake by each sister, and by the time they got to whoever went third, the guests would be bored and that poor sister would miss out.

Ah, the tiny and yet huge problems of a triple wedding.

Brooke had already booked the Wedlock Creek Chapel for the June wedding the triplets wanted, as well as the grand ballroom of the Wellington Hotel. She had set up tastings at seven caterers, all of whom offered a gluten-free menu, and had gotten live club dates for five of the bands on the list so that the triplets could see how they performed live. The sisters had been Pinteresting their wedding gowns and bridesmaid dresses for years now, well before they'd ever met their fiancés, so they were all now on special order. Each group of bridesmaids would wear a slightly different hue of pink. The entire wedding party, including the brides, would wear cowboy boots—stiletto-versions for the triplets.

Gram, you would have gotten such a kick out of this wedding, she thought with a smile.

After her work was done, Nick kept popping into her mind. She was dying to know how things were going at the party. She thought of him in that dark suit...and saw herself walking down an aisle to her waiting groom. To Nick Garroway.

Her breath hitched.

"Okay, boys. Time for a stroll. Maybe a trip to Java Jane's for a blast of caffeine for mama." She got Mikey and Morgan in their stroller and headed out, the sun still so bright at five thirty, the summer air warm and breezy and smelling like her neighbor's gorgeous rose garden.

In five minutes she was at the coffee shop, eyeing the slices of chocolate cheesecake and hoping the line would move quickly, when she felt a tap on her shoulder.

"Brooke Timber, right?" the woman asked, flashing very white teeth in a faux smile that didn't reach her eyes.

Interesting, Brooke thought. "That's me."

"I'm Allison Fielding of the newly opened Weddings by Allison. I heard you were my biggest competition."

Brooke laughed. "Well, I guess I should take that as a compliment, considering there are several wedding planners in Wedlock Creek. Welcome."

Allison didn't even bother with a smile. "I also heard you just signed the Satler triplets' wedding. Quite a coup."

"I'm enjoying planning the wedding. Lots of balls to keep in the air," Brooke said, something in the woman's tone making her wary.

"Yes. I know a wedding planner in Jackson who planned a twin wedding, and boy, did that turn into a disaster," Allison said. "The twins were at each other's throats, couldn't agree on anything, and my poor friend took the brunt of their anger and all the blame. She ended up having to move, poor thing. And you've got *triplets*."

Ah. Brooke knew this game. It was called I'm Trying To Psych You Out. But Allison Fielding clearly didn't know Brooke well.

"Well, I've got this," Brooke said, inching up in the line. "If I can singlehandedly raise twins and run a successful business, I can do anything. At least that's what I tell myself," she added so she wouldn't be completely fibbing.

Allison's gloating expression turned into a bit of a scowl before she caught herself. "Well, good luck. You'll need it."

"Actually, what I need is experience, passion and being good at what I do, and I've got all three covered, so I'll be just fine. But thanks."

Luckily Brooke had reached the counter, so she added a smile and turned back around to the barista.

The amazing thing was that, a week ago, this conversation would have derailed Brooke for the day, made her anxious and worried, and left her wondering if she *did* have what it took. But even before Nick Garroway, Wonder Manny, had come into her life, she'd gone after the Satlers' business and she'd made it work.

Yeah, fine, maybe they would have run screaming out of her office if he hadn't shown up just when he had. But she'd had them until that moment, and they'd known that she "got" them, knew what they wanted and would make the entire planning of the huge affair easier on all three. Even if they had gone racing out to save themselves from the hint of baby poop in the air, they would have come back. She believed that.

Because she was good at what she did. Her grandmother had taught her everything she knew. So take that, Ms. High-and-Mighty and—

"Hi, Brooke. Small iced coffee?" the barista asked.

"You know what? I'll take a large iced mocha. With whipped cream. And a slice of the chocolate cheesecake." She'd been dreaming of that frothy drink for months. And now that she'd landed a big account, why not celebrate a little?

I have my mojo back, she realized with a little thrill. *Hear that, Gram?* she thought, picturing Aggie Timber's lively, animated face and her signature chignon and colorful pantsuits. *I've got this. Dream Weddings is going to be more than fine.*

As she moved over to wait for her order, the word *celebration* echoed in her mind. She wondered how things were going for Nick at the Garroway Paper party. She hoped his brother wasn't being the equivalent of Allison Fielding, but she had a feeling he was.

Over the next bunch of days, Brooke couldn't help but notice that Nick had made himself scarce, which was difficult to do in a small house. He appeared like clockwork at 9:00 a.m., ready to take charge of the twins, and then reappeared at 1:00 p.m., with them changed, fed and ready for a trip to see their favorite squirrels. He'd text throughout the day.

Let me know if you need a break or some time to work. I'm here for you.

And her heart would clench. He was here for her but didn't want to be—that was what she was finally realizing. He was acting in good faith because of the promise, but he wanted to be anywhere but here.

The only place he'd rather be even less than here was anywhere his brother was. Ever since Nick had returned from Garroway Paper's fortieth-anniversary party, he'd been distant, both emotionally and otherwise. Except when it came to the twins. Even if he was faking it with them, he'd smile and come alive, with his voice animated and his hugs full of emotion. The cats seemed to cheer him up some too. She'd often find Nick sitting on the patio, deep in thought, with Snowball on his lap and Smudge wedged between his ankles.

And sometimes she'd think, *Well, maybe he does want to be here. Maybe it's just his family giving him agita and grief.* But he seemed to be avoiding her too.

Told you not to get all emotionally involved with him! she mentally yelled at herself. But today was Friday and they were leaving for the Sagebrush Sanctuary and Retreat tonight—and staying in the same suite. Which should feel no different than home, really. They'd have their own bedrooms and schedules. He'd probably avoid her there too.

Their group would stay until Sunday morning, and see the newlyweds off on their honeymoon for a week in London. The owner of Sagebrush, a very calm-sounding woman named Geraldine, had assured her that her daughter, who was working part-time at the center for the summer, would babysit the twins for all of the major activities—tonight's rehearsal dinner, wedding prep and the wedding itself late tomorrow afternoon. Everything was all set. On the home front, Cathy had hired a trusted dogsitter to take in Fritz for the weekend, and a neighbor's teenaged daughter would pop in three times a day to play with Snowball and Smudge and keep their food and water bowls clean and full.

Nick came downstairs with their suitcases and the twins' bag, and then he started packing up his Jeep. They settled Morgan and Mikey in their rear-facing car seats and Nick put the lullaby player on low for them.

"I was thinking today about how crazy things are," he said as they got inside and buckled up.

"Crazy?" she asked. Her feelings for him were crazy, but she had a gorgeous, sexy, six-foot-two-inch manny whose presence in her life was the first bit of absolute magic she'd experienced outside of the birth of her children. He made things less crazy in that regard.

"We're going to a wedding. My dad's. Your client's. At a yoga retreat. When I was driving from the Texas base to Wedlock Creek, I never could have imagined what was in store. Crazy."

"Ah, so good-crazy, really."

He smiled. "I guess so. Unexpected."

Oh yes. Very unexpected. Every bit of how life had unfolded since Nick Garroway's arrival in her life. "Definitely unexpected. Which is why we're headed to the right place to just relax a little. The country, nature, trees, winding paths, good energy and healthy foods. Sagebrush Sanctuary and Retreat is much more than a yoga retreat—it's a wellness center. The focus is on healing, whatever that word means to a particular person at that particular moment in his or her life."

"I don't think staring at trees or eating hummus is going to heal me," he said with something of a smile. "Cynical, I know, but I'm not one to stare off into the middle distance."

"We'll just see, then." She'd been to a couple of wellness centers with her grandmother, and if he thought looking at trees wouldn't help, he was about to find out how wrong he was. Nature, with very little else to distract, had a way of calming a person like nothing else could. You could think, listen to yourself and come up with answers when none had seemed forthcoming.

She could do with some tree-staring herself.

"What are the accommodations?" he asked. "Is it like a lodge? Or are there individual cabins?"

"Our yurt is a suite. That way we can both have easy

access to the twins when we're not at the rehearsal dinner or the wedding."

"Wait, a yurt? Like a tent-and-cabin one?"

"Yup. There are some traditional cabins and rooms in the main lodge, but they were all booked. The wedding party will be staying in the yurts, and most of the guests are just driving in for the wedding and leaving afterward, since it's over by ten."

"Brandon should love staying in a yurt," he said. He smiled at the thought, and so did Brooke.

If you don't ask, you don't get info that you're dying to know, she reminded herself. Sometimes a little prying was good. Nick had evaded her questions over the last couple of days, but maybe getting him to open up, even just a little now, would help with some of his tension.

She glanced at him. "Have you spoken to your brother since the party at Garroway Paper?"

All she knew of that day was that Nick "didn't want to talk about it," so she assumed Brandon had ratcheted up the pressure on getting Nick to work for the company. Or maybe his dad had too, but Brooke didn't get the feeling that Jeb was after Nick to work for the family business. Brooke had the feeling that his dad had come to some good conclusions about Nick going his own way.

And she also had a feeling that unexpectedly finding love—a second chance at happiness with another person—had a lot to do with that.

"He emailed me a bunch of documents the night of the party," Nick said. "Financials, company overview, five-year plan. He even included a speech he'd given at some conference about his favorite kind of paper. You should have heard the passion in his voice about brightness and opacity and coatings."

"Sounds like he really cares about paper too," Brooke said.

"Wish I did."

She looked at him, tilting her head. "Do you really?"

He nodded. "If I cared an eighth as much about paper as they did, I'd probably want to join the business. But I don't care about paper, Brooke. And that pits me against my family. It would be like if you didn't care about weddings."

"I think my grandmother would have been all right with me following my own passions though."

"After showing you the ropes? Working at her side since you were knee-high?"

She bit her lip. "Yeah, maybe she would have been a little disappointed that her company wouldn't go on. But I think she'd want me to be happy. She wouldn't want her happiness at my expense. That's not love."

He glanced at her. "Brandon doesn't look at it that way. It's not about happiness or giving up anything. It's about doing what's right. To him anyway."

"Do you think you two will be able to build a new relationship?"

"I don't know. I don't see how."

"It kills you, doesn't it," she said in almost a whisper.

"Yeah. It does. He's my kid brother, even if he's twenty-seven now. I was once everything to him. Now he sees me as a disappointment. I didn't realize how much that bothered me until I got here and started interacting with him."

"Maybe this weekend, two families coming together, a show of love, will help. And all the nature and yurts."

That got a smile out of him. "I hope so, Brooke. But I won't hold my breath."

I will, she thought. *If not for the two of you, then for the two of us.* But maybe that was just as hopeless. Nick could see how stubborn his brother was being, but he couldn't see how stubborn he himself was being. At his own expense. Denying himself love because of the past. Looking to run off to the Wyoming wilderness, hours away, to avoid everything.

She needed this weekend to work on him too.

She *would* hold her breath.

Chapter Nine

Nick liked the yurts. They were like round cabin-tents but looked more like cabins than tents. Certainly not military tents. Painted a robin's-egg blue with many large windows, and sparsely decorated with floor cushions and futons for beds, the yurts were cozy and welcoming. There were ten yurts in their part of the sanctuary, each with its own private bathroom, which Nick was glad to see.

Just across the path was a meditation center, a long, rectangular, open-air structure with billowy white sheer fabric draped and silver yoga mats on the polished bamboo floor. Nestled behind the meditation center, in a clearing in the woods, was a gazebo currently decorated for the Garroway-Wylie wedding ceremony. White roses—hundreds of them—were entwined across the

top and sides of the gazebo, with a pale green runner
stretching from the gazebo to one of the smaller yurts,
which was where the wedding party would gather until
it was time to walk down the aisle.

Their group had this part of the sanctuary to themselves. According to Brooke, there were four groupings
for large gatherings and parties, each at enough of a distance to make everyone feel the place was theirs alone.
A river flowed across the entire length of the sanctuary; Nick could see parts of it that weren't blocked by
flowering bushes and leafy trees.

He had to admit, it was all very nice, and probably nothing at all like his father's first nuptials, which
according to his mother had been a very traditional
church wedding, followed by a reception at an Italian
restaurant.

Nick glanced at the silver mats in the living room
area of the suite he'd be sharing with Brooke and the
twins. "Am I expected to meditate?"

Brooke smiled. "All you *have* to do is show up for
the wedding. Nothing else."

"Huh. I like that. No pressure." The moment the word
pressure had come out of his mouth, he realized he was
wound up so tightly, he was surprised he didn't explode.
But it was different from the pressure he'd felt when
he'd arrived back in Wedlock Creek. Then, the buildup
of his stomach acids and the tightening of his chest had
been about something as simple, as ordinary, as stepping foot back in his hometown. And then there was
the promise to the man who'd saved his life, to check
on a woman named Brooke Timber.

Nick remembered when Will Parker had returned

from a leave and shown his tent mates the photo of the woman he'd met back home. Everyone had said she was gorgeous, and Will had put his phone away without lingering on Brooke's picture or staring at it for an hour like Nick would have done if she'd been his woman. If he'd met Brooke Timber, if he'd touched her, made love to her, and then had her photo on his phone, it would be his lifeline, his link to home—and that word would have mattered. The word *home* would have meant something other than heartache and pain and grief.

Brooke was special.

"No pressure," she repeated, but he barely heard her because he was caught on the word in his head. *Special. Special. Special.* "That's what a wellness retreat is about. Relaxing your way."

Nick sat down on the rattan love seat. A pitcher of fruit-infused water was on the coffee table. He poured two glasses and handed one to Brooke.

Yes, so Brooke was special. Special, period. And special to *him.*

She drank some. "Delicious."

He took a sip. It was crazy that they were talking water when he'd just come to the most amazing realization,

That Brooke had truly managed to work her way in past some of his defenses. Others were still up, as usual, fighting the good fight against anything that could do damage.

"Twins asleep?" he asked, needing some distraction from his thoughts. His crazy wayward thoughts. Okay, so she was special. What did that really mean? What was he going to do about it? If anything.

He could let up a little and see about giving the attraction between them a chance.

She nodded. "They seem to like their yurt crib." The mini futon lining the wooden crib was covered in a soft material, and the lullaby player they'd brought played a soft melody. Nick would have fallen asleep in that room if he weren't so wide awake. At being here with Brooke in this strange place. At being here with his family.

"So, here's the agenda for tonight," she said, sitting down beside him. He could smell the hint of perfume she always wore. He suddenly wanted *them* to be on the agenda. But at the same time, his feelings—ugh, he hated using that word—felt so...raw and new. It was probably best to let things happen naturally and not announce what she already knew: that he had a thing for her. He'd told her as much and then said in the same breath that he didn't want to and wouldn't do anything about it.

That had changed and yet hadn't...not completely.

One day at a time. One hour at a time. One moment at a time. Wasn't that the physical-rehabilitation center's motto?

"The rehearsal dinner will start at six thirty. The center's owner's daughter will babysit for us. She'll be here in a little over an hour."

He nodded. That was the second time he and Brooke were expected somewhere together, and the notion felt...right, as though they were a pair.

"Well, I'll go shower and change," he said, grateful for the getaway, for the chance to be alone with his all-over-the-place thoughts. "Then I'll bring the twins into my room, and you can get ready. I'll just need five minutes."

"Nice to be a man," she said with a grin.

"Brooke Timber, you could step out of the shower, put on your clothes and walk out the door and be as gorgeous as if you got all style-y with your hair and put on makeup. And that's a fact."

She held his gaze for a moment, as if touched by the compliment. "Well, I appreciate that you think so, but nah."

He smiled and went into his bedroom and sank down on the all-white bed, thinking of Brooke stepping naked and damp out of the shower.

What was going on in his brain? *Go with it, or don't go with it. Leave her alone, or don't leave her alone. Act on your feelings—or don't.*

He didn't know what was right. He didn't know where his own head was.

Another silver yoga mat was by the window, and the breezy July evening air was gently blowing the gauzy curtains. He lay down on the mat and fully stretched out, then closed his eyes, and his brain almost exploded. He bolted up.

So much for meditation. Then again, he was probably doing it wrong. He hadn't been doing much of anything; he'd just lain down and closed his eyes, and a bunch of images had shot at him: Elena slamming the door in his face; Aisha's round dark eyes embedded in his mind's eye; Will Parker yelling and diving on top of him; the torturer of a physical therapist who'd actually done wonders on his leg; and Nick's name on a magnetic placard on an office at Garroway Paper.

Over the past few months, Nick had had some nightmares about the first three. But it had been his name on that office door that had done him in this time and made him sit up, sweat breaking out on his forehead.

This was the guy he was going to present to Brooke as a possibility for the future she wanted? Really? And what? Now he was throwing around the word *future*? A minute ago he'd been wondering about giving their attraction a chance. Big jump from that to the future.

One thing at a time, one moment at a time, he reminded himself.

He'd have to ask someone about meditating. Maybe there was supposed to be chanting or holding his fingers a certain way or sitting cross-legged.

He got up and sucked down half a glass of the fruit-infused water on his nightstand, then opened his suitcase on his bed. Brooke had given him a brief list of what to pack, since he had no idea what a yurt-yoga-wellness wedding would require, other than the suit he'd already bought for the wedding itself. The dress code for the weekend was "fancy beach-esque," and he'd had to ask Brooke what that meant. Apparently it meant a white linen shirt, sleeves rolled up, top two buttons undone and linen trousers with the cuffs rolled to the ankles. Loafers. No socks. He'd had to go buy all that, since he owned nothing made of linen, and he'd last had loafers in middle school.

He took a quick shower in the tiny, narrow private bathroom attached to his room, which helped get his head back on straight, and was drying off with the fluffy white towel and about to shave when he thought he heard one of the twins let out a cry. He stepped out of his room, into the main area, an ear peeled toward Brooke's bedroom right next door. She must have heard his shower shut off, because she turned hers on.

Waah-waah!

Yup, a crier. With the shower going, he couldn't tell which one it was. He waited a beat. More crying. He tied his towel more firmly above his hips, then went in, figuring he'd take out the crier so that Brooke could shower and get ready in peace. And just as he had Mikey in his arms, Brooke came out of her bathroom, barely wrapped in a white towel herself.

He stared at her.

She stared at him.

"I thought I heard one of them," she stammered, her gaze moving all over the place—up, down, anywhere but his eyes. He could barely handle looking at her straight on too. There was so little between them— two fluffy towels—and the possibility of sex, that he couldn't think straight.

Just walk out of her room, he told himself.

But he didn't.

He hoisted Mikey higher in his arms and walked over to Brooke, who was now looking him in the eyes. And he leaned forward and kissed her—a warm, hard, passionate kiss that summed up everything he felt at the moment, whether he'd meant to express that or not. More than desire. More than just caring about her. Much, much more than just fulfilling a promise.

She let out a small gasp and kissed him back, then turned and quickly shut herself in her bathroom.

He smiled and headed out of the room with Mikey.

"At least your mama and I are both on the same

page," he told the little guy. "The step forward and the step backward."

"Ga da," Mikey said, grabbing his still-damp chin.

"Ga da, is right." Nick let out a breath, gently swaying Mikey, wondering just what tonight was going to bring. After the dinner. When he and Brooke would return to their suite. If he touched her, if the "towels" came off, then he'd have to be ready to commit to Brooke and her twins. One guy had already hurt her in that department, and there was no way in hell Nick would do the same. That would be the opposite of the promise he'd made.

Will we or won't we? Should I or shouldn't I?

He had a feeling he'd only know in the moment. But if he *shouldn't*, then the "moment," which would entail taking another step backward, would do a lot of damage between them.

"Feelings are complicated, Mikey," he whispered to the baby, breathing in the baby-shampoo scent of him.

"Ba ga," was all Mikey would say on the matter.

"I'd like to make a toast to my dad and Cathy at the wedding tomorrow," Brandon said, and all eyes turned to him at the long wooden table set up in the meditation room for the rehearsal dinner. Tomorrow this structure would serve as the reception site and be full of six round tables.

The rehearsal dinner was just immediate family, a small group—Cathy and Jeb, the Garroway brothers, Cathy's two daughters, Lyndsey and Nina, and Brooke with her electronic notes and old-fashioned little planner.

Brandon glanced around the table. "I know the wedding came together very quickly, so this subject didn't come up—or maybe it didn't for other reasons—but I'd like a minute allotted for a toast to the happy couple."

Brooke groaned inwardly. The subject hadn't come up for those "other reasons," but not just the one that Brandon was likely referring to. Brooke had called both of Cathy's daughters to ask if they'd like to speak at the ceremony, whether to give a speech or read a poem or sing a song—anything they wanted—and both daughters had said they loved their mother to pieces but they were way too shy and reserved for that. Having spent the last half hour in their company, she would agree with that. Nineteen and twenty-one, both students in pastry school, they were very polite and doted on their mother, but both were on the quiet side.

On the drive here, she'd asked Nick if he wanted to say a few words at the ceremony, and he shook his head and said he'd put his well-wishes into a card—the entire left side filled out with how glad he was to be back in his father's life and how he wished all the happiness in the world to Jeb and Cathy. Brooke had been touched by that. Since three fourths of the bride's and groom's offspring had said no to speaking, Brooke had hoped to cross "speeches" off her list. Still, on the off chance Brandon wanted to give a toast, she'd planned to speak to him about it before the rehearsal dinner, so they could factor it in, but after that kiss…a lot had gone *whoosh* out of her head.

She mentally slapped a palm to her head. A wedding planner could not get sidetracked or distracted, especially by her own personal life, at the eleventh hour, and a rehearsal dinner was exactly that. She had to keep her focus on the details. Tomorrow all the deliveries would start arriving, and she'd be running around with her lists and her phone to her ear, making sure everything was perfect and as Cathy, her bride and client, wished. Luckily the events manager, a pretty young woman named Heather, was very attentive and take-charge.

That was what she had to do—focus on her job, not her lips and how much they craved more of Nick's. But *oh*, that kiss. There had been so much packed into it that, when she'd fled back into the bathroom, she'd had to sit down and catch her breath and go over everything that had been inside it. How could so much be inside one kiss? She'd felt his desire, but even more she felt how much she meant to him. That had been what had sent her scurrying for cover behind closed doors.

Because once again she'd been struck by the notion that he was in her life to fulfill that promise, not because he was falling in love with her. Maybe she'd just straight out ask him.

Nick, I can tell you care about me. But do you simply feel responsible for me, or do you love me?

Why couldn't she imagine him saying, "Brooke, I love you"?

Because he probably didn't know how he felt. He'd dealt with some emotional whoppers in his past. And everything was tangled up for him right now, his brother's pressure like the ole albatross around his neck, making everything else feel off balance too. Brooke had the feeling Nick was questioning himself. And she was sure that she and the twins factored in that questioning. *Do I? Don't I?* Then a flinging of hands in the air.

He very likely didn't know how he truly felt about her. He didn't know anything that was going on in that long-guarded heart of his. That, she'd bank on.

"If you could give me an estimate of how long you'd like for your toast, Brandon," Brooke said, "I'll factor it in for before the ceremony."

"Excellent," he said. "I've learned while speaking in public for Garroway Paper that a minute is a longer time than anyone realizes. I doubt I'll need more than forty-five seconds."

She glanced at Nick. He pulled at the collar of his shirt.

"I'd like to say a few words too," Nick said, surprising the heck out of her. "Twenty seconds," he added to Brooke.

She smiled and made some notations in her planner.

"Well, if the sons are speaking, we should speak too," Cathy's daughter Nina said, looking at her sister. The Wylie daughters had barely said ten words so far, but she was glad Nina had spoken up.

"We can read something, right?" Lyndsey asked. "It doesn't have to come off the top our heads?"

"Yes," Brooke assured her. "A short poem, a song or a short toast you write and read. Anything you want."

The sisters decided they would share the reading of a favorite love poem.

"I'm so happy!" Cathy said, leaning over to give each of her daughters a hug.

Jeb, meanwhile, sent nods of approval to both of his sons, and for the first time she'd known this group, everyone looked comfortable and happy.

"Perfect," Brooke said. And huh. Who would have

thought that Brandon Garroway would have been responsible for getting his brother and Cathy's daughters to stand up and give toasts at the wedding? She sent Brandon a smile and made note to talk to him privately later and thank him for teaching her a lesson. She'd figured that with three of the four "kids" not giving toasts, that one getting up to speak would call attention to the three who'd declined. But instead all four would be participating. And she knew that would make Jeb and Cathy happy. *Go, Brandon*, she thought.

As the waiter assigned to them cleared the table, their group moved over to the gazebo to go over where they'd stand for the ceremony and the basic setup.

The minister was due to meet them any minute, and Brooke could see her coming down the path with Heather, the events manager. Heather put her hands in prayer formation and said, "Namaste." Then Cathy made the introductions of the minister to the group.

"Namaste," Brandon repeated, more to himself, and Brooke glanced over to find him staring in absolute awe at Heather.

Brooke had to smile. Heather, a very pretty woman in her midtwenties, didn't immediately look like Brandon's type—not that Brooke had any idea what that was. He was so buttoned-up and black-and-white that she couldn't see him falling for a woman with two braids wrapped around the sides of her head like Princess Leia, with white flowers woven inside. She wore a long, flowy outfit in keeping with "beach-fancy" and seemed remarkably poised and at peace while being extremely efficient when it came to her job. Brandon still hadn't taken his eyes off her.

But then Heather was heading back to the main lodge, and the minister was talking about the ceremony and the vows and scheduling in the four new speakers.

"Guess I have homework tonight," Nick whispered. "To figure out what I'm going to say."

Brooke smiled—with relief. Maybe he'd be too busy working on his toast to bring up the kiss. Or do it again.

She honestly wasn't sure if she was glad about that or not.

Chapter Ten

In the yurt-suite's living room, Nick sat on the love seat, with a pad of paper on his lap that he was tapping a pen against. Four wadded-up paper balls were on the floor around him. Yeah, this wasn't going well. *Thanks, Brandon*, he thought, rolling his eyes, but he meant that *thanks* both sarcastically and not.

A wordsmith, Nick wasn't. He'd managed to eke out some heartfelt congratulations and best wishes in the wedding card he'd bought, but writing that was easy— no one was staring at him and hearing his words while he filled out the card. This was something else entirely.

Brooke glanced at the floor and his crumpled papers. "Need some help? I've only heard five thousand wedding toasts in the past several years."

What he would give to toss the pad and pick up

Brooke instead and sweep her into one of the bedrooms. The kiss they'd shared came roaring back to him, and his nerve endings were on red alert. How good she'd felt and smelled and tasted.

Except he couldn't do any of that and she was waiting for an answer to a simple question.

"Everything I start to write sounds so canned and clichéd, the usual stuff," he said, ripping off the page and crumpling it and sending it to join its fellow pathetic attempts. "I'm not trying to be Shakespeare, but I want to sound like I mean what I'm saying."

She sat down across from him, on one of the round floor cushions. "It's a small wedding—barely forty people. Family and friends and coworkers coming in tomorrow. These are the people who truly know your dad and Cathy, so you might as well speak from the heart."

"Give me a first line," he said, knowing he was cheating.

She grinned, but then her expression became more wistful as she stared out the window, clearly deep in thought. She turned back to him. "Okay, I've got your first line. 'My dad and I haven't always been close.'"

His stomach clenched. "I don't know…"

"Your reaction, Nick? It's called honesty. And that's what you're going for. Authenticity. Being here, among all this nature, somehow asks that. I think that's why you have so many crumpled pages."

"I don't want to say a bunch of canned lines, but I don't know how authentic I want to get either," Nick admitted. Opening up a can of honesty could let out who-knew-what.

"Well, humor me, then. 'My dad and I haven't always been close,'" she repeated. "What would your next line be?"

He didn't even hesitate before saying, "But I think we're on our way." His eyes widened as the lightbulb above his head dinged on.

She smiled. "My work here is done."

"My dad and I haven't always been close," he said slowly as he wrote it down. "But I think we're on our way. Nothing would make me happier—except maybe seeing how happy my father is because Cathy is in his life. The way the two of them interact makes me feel that anything is possible."

He glanced at Brooke to see if she liked the track he was on, and there were tears in her eyes. He stood up and walked over to her. "Hey, what's wrong?"

"You really mean that." She sniffled. "I know you do."

"Yeah, I do," he said, using the back of his thumb to wipe away the dusting of tears under her eyes.

"That's how I feel when I'm with you," she whispered. "Like anything is possible."

His first thought was absolutely nothing as a rush of what sounded like the roar of ocean waves filled his head. And then he heard himself say, "Me too."

And then he did pick her up and carry her into his bedroom, using a foot to swipe his overnight bag off the bed. He laid her down and kissed her as he stretched out on top of her. "Should we do this, Brooke?"

"We should," she whispered, putting her hands in his hair. "Damn the torpedoes, right?"

He pulled up a bit, propping himself on his elbows, and put her face in his hands. "No," he whispered back.

"Not right. I can't let myself touch you if I think I might hurt you. I made that promise to myself—and to you."

"So, the promise evolved?" she asked, the tears shimmering in her eyes again.

"Yes. A while ago." As he looked at her, he could feel his heart cracking open just enough to make him realize he felt more for her than he'd even realized. She'd gotten *way* deep inside where he thought he'd closed himself off.

"Forget the torpedoes," she said. "Let's just see what happens. That's all we can do."

He barely felt himself nodding, then reached for his wallet and pulled out a foil-wrapped packet. "This has been in here for over a year, but I'm glad I never chucked it." He set it down on the bedside table so that it would be at the ready.

She smiled. "So am I."

And then somehow she'd managed to flip him over so that she was on top of him. As she left a trail of kisses along his neck and collarbone, he closed his eyes, loath not to look at her, but the sensations were so overwhelming that he couldn't help it.

And then piece by piece, the beach-fancy wear came off and Nick Garroway lost all ability to think at all.

Brooke woke up just after midnight but kept her eyes closed in case everything that had happened earlier was a dream. She opened one eye and turned her head slightly to the right. Nope, not a dream. Nick Garroway was really beside her—naked, the quilt starting around his hips or so. For a moment she let herself fully appreciate his chest, so strong and muscled, his rippled arms a sight to behold. He had a small tattoo on his left bicep—purple mountains. From the patriotic song, she figured.

She watched his chest rise and fall, rise and fall, rise and fall, and instead of snuggling close beside him, reliving every delicious moment of their time together in this bed, her own chest tightened. He'd said the promise had evolved, that he wouldn't touch her if he couldn't do so without hurting her. But how could he make that promise? How could he know how he'd feel down the road, when he suddenly wouldn't be the manny but her *man*...and father figure—or even father—to her children.

Based on all he'd said, all he was going through, Nick was in flux. Adjusting to civilian life in this unlikely temporary job, killing two birds with one stone by easing into that new life and making good on the promise he'd made to the fallen soldier who'd saved his life. It was a very effective way to say goodbye to his military service in the most honorable way. She had a feeling that was why Nick had settled in so well, so easily. Because it felt right to him.

But he'd never planned on anything happening between the two of them. In fact he'd said, loud and clear, that it couldn't happen. Enter chemistry and attraction and their lives intermingling in this crazy way, with her planning his father's wedding, and yadda, yadda, yadda, they were in bed right now.

Granted, he was sleeping—soundly. So something must be all right for him.

Yeah, dumbbell, she chastised herself. *He just had*

sex. Of course he was sound asleep. Of course all was well for him. *Now.*

Just wait till his eyes opened. And the bright light of day had its way with him.

That was what she was afraid of. That he meant everything he said last night—and that he'd mean everything he felt in the morning.

Her chest tightened again. She needed air. She needed to go stare at some trees. She grabbed his yellow pad and scrawled a note, that it was—she glanced at the analog clock on the wall—12:04 a.m. and she was taking a walk along the river and would be back in a half hour.

Then she quickly dressed in yoga pants and a long T-shirt, threw her hair into a ponytail, slipped into her sneakers, and checked on the twins in her bedroom—fast asleep.

"I made you two a promise myself," she whispered to her boys. "That everything I'd do would be for you." *Falling for Nick in the hopes that he would join our family would be one of the best things I could do for you two*, she thought, running a light hand over Morgan's fine brown wispy curls and then Mikey's impossibly soft cheek. *But getting my heart smashed when he leaves instead will only make me an unfocused mess, and I need to be fully present for you two. I'm all you have.*

Oh God. She *was* all they had. For real. This was no newsflash, of course, but the reality of it blinked in neon above their cribs.

There would be no smashed heart. She simply couldn't allow it to happen. She had a business to run and children to raise, and letting herself be at the mercy of a broken heart went against every bit of the promise she'd made. She knew because she'd been there when Will had ghosted her: that state of turmoil, the checking of her email and phone for texts constantly, the anxiety. And when she wrote him that she was pregnant—with twins—and his response was to say sorry but no? She'd been a mess for months.

Then again, she'd been facing motherhood alone, with her beloved gram gone. She'd been so scared. Now she was firmly on her feet. She knew what she was capable of. She'd be fine. But not if she walked into the path of a steam engine in the form of a six-foot-two-inch former soldier who cooked and cleaned and changed diapers and hummed lullabies and told stories. And made love like every fantasy she'd ever had.

Air. Tree-staring. Pronto.

Brooke quietly left the yurt and glanced around—not a soul to be seen. It was so quiet. The sanctuary was such a distance from the nearest town that it would be unlikely that anyone would be lurking around, except a coyote. She'd watch out for those.

She headed down the path past the meditation center, past the beautiful gazebo and toward the river. Just the sound of the gentle whoosh helped steady her. *Breathe in, breathe out, Brooke.*

Someone was sitting on a big flat-topped rock by the riverbank, with an elbow on one knee, and tossing small rocks in the water. Who was that? She stepped a bit closer and saw the dark hair, the back of the white

linen shirt and pants like his brother's, and she knew it
was Brandon Garroway.

"Hi," she called out.

He bolted up and turned around, his expression going
from hopeful excitement to disappointment. "Oh, hi,
Brooke."

Interesting. Who did he think she was at first?

"*Oh, hi* sounds like you were hoping I'd be someone else." She recalled the way he'd looked at Heather,
the sanctuary's events manager, earlier, and wondered
if they'd made a midnight rendezvous that she hadn't
shown up for. Brooke must be more of a romantic than
she thought, because what was the likelihood of that?

"That obvious, huh?" he asked, his voice a bit mopey.

"*Were* you meeting someone?" she asked.

He sighed and returned to his spot on the rock. "In
one of those crazy things that could only happen at a
yoga wellness sanctuary in the middle of the Wyoming
wilderness, I met someone."

Aha! She knew it. And yup, she was definitely a romantic. Could a wedding planner be otherwise?

"Heather?" she asked, joining him on the rock, her
feet dangling.

He gaped at her, "How'd you know?"

"I couldn't help but notice the way you looked at her
when she brought over the minister earlier."

He stared at the river, then glanced at Brooke. "I'm
not surprised it showed on my face. I've never experienced anything like that before. I mean, I've looked at
women and thought, 'Wow, she's very pretty,' but I've
never looked at someone and thought, 'I'm going to
marry this woman.'"

Now she gaped at him. "Seriously?"

"I guess this love-at-first-sight thing is real. I always thought it was nonsense. And I can't make heads or tails of it. I felt this instant connection, instant attraction, instant chemistry—before she even said a word. How is that possible? Is it just because I think she's beautiful?"

She smiled—gently. "I'm sure it's everything you just said—the instant connection. It's powerful but it's real. And it hit you."

"Hard," he said, nodding.

"So, you were supposed to meet here but she didn't turn up?"

"More like we did meet here, at eleven, when she was completely off duty from leading a bedtime meditation session, but the conversation took an unexpected turn and she ran off. She told me not to follow her. So I just stayed here, hoping she'd come back."

Oh boy. "What happened? If you don't mind my asking?"

He bit his lip. "No, I'm glad you're here. I could really use someone to talk to."

She hugged her knees to her chest, glad her own issues were far, far away at the moment.

Brandon ran a hand through his hair, hanging his head back for a moment. "I told her how I felt, that it was insane and made no sense, that I was a by-the-book, numbers-and-facts-oriented person and ran a company, but I saw her and knew I was going to marry her."

Brooke smiled. "You told her that?"

He nodded. "Sure did. She looked at me like I was nuts, so I said, 'I'm hoping that we can at least go on a date, so that no matter what happens, if you're not interested, not attracted, if you hate me within ten minutes, I'll know I tried.'"

Huh. Even Brooke would have gone for that. Not bad, Brandon. "I'll bet she said yes to that."

"She gave me the most dazzling smile, said she'd meet me at eleven at the flat-topped rock behind the meditation center, but that I 'should know this—things aren't always what they seem.'"

Brooke tilted her head. "What did that mean?"

"Oh, trust me, I paced around my yub-cabin—or whatever it's called—for two hours, wondering that very thing. Finally, at ten thirty, I had to get out of that weird circular hotel-room thing, and I waited here for her. She came, looking even more beautiful than before."

Brooke thought of Heather with her Princess Leia braids and flowy layers. She smiled, appreciating this side of Brandon. Who knew? People were complicated, never all this or all that. "So, what wasn't what it seemed?" Brooke asked.

He let out a deep breath and looked skyward before turning his gaze on the river. "Turns out she's three months pregnant. She told the father, and he accused her of trying to pin it on him because he had a motorboat. That was a month ago and he disappeared on her. She thinks he left the state."

Brooke sighed. "There's a little too much of that going around."

"What do you mean?"

"Same thing happened to me," Brooke explained. "With a soldier, home on leave. I thought we had something special, but turns out I was just temporarily special."

"A soldier? Wait—my brother? Nick's the father of the twins? No wonder he's the manny. Now it all makes sense. Sort of."

Brooke shook her head. "No, no, no. He's not their father." She told him the whole story, starting with almost losing the Satler triplets to Nick bursting in and explaining why he'd come, to having the best nanny that ever existed. She left out the more personal details.

"Wow," Brandon said. "I'm surprised he even bothered making good on that promise. He certainly didn't think he owed his family anything."

Oh Lord. "A soldier died saving Nick's life and asked for a favor. Of course he was going to make it happen."

"I guess…when you put it like that," Brandon agreed.

Brooke glanced away so she could roll her eyes as hard as she needed to.

"Think you two will get married?" Brandon asked.

She coughed on air. "Why would you say that?"

"Oh, come on. You think it's not obvious there's something between you two?"

She'd seen big-time emotion, clear as day, on Brandon's face earlier; it made sense that others would see *feeling* in her expression too. And maybe Nick's. He was more unreadable. "Well, whatever's between us is complicated. Let's just leave it at that."

"Complicated. That's the word of the day. I definitely wasn't expecting Heather to tell me she was pregnant. And do you want to know the craziest part of all?"

Brooke looked at him.

"That she's pregnant doesn't change how I feel about

her. She's the woman I'm going to marry. I just know it. Turns out the baby I saw far off in my future will come sooner than I figured—I was thinking a few years down the road, but hey, life happens."

"It sure does," Brooke agreed—in absolute wonder that she was having this conversation with Brandon Garroway. "So, why did she run off?"

He let out another breath. "I explained that her being pregnant didn't change a thing for me. And she said it might not today or in a few weeks, but when the reality hit, I'd be gone. I insisted that would never happen, to give me a chance to show her, and she shook her head and ran off and told me not to follow."

Brooke bit her lip. Hadn't she had this very conversation with herself, in bed, with Nick sleeping beside her? "She was probably overwhelmed. You must have seemed like Prince Charming falling from the sky, and her life likely doesn't feel like a fairy tale, you know?"

Which could apply to her and Nick. He was like her own Prince Charming and Mary Poppins rolled into one. Temporarily anyway.

"I think I do," he said. "So, do I storm the castle?"

Brooke laughed. "Nah. Not tonight. Talk to her tomorrow morning and let her know that you'd like to get to know her, for her to get to know you, and all you're asking for is a chance. That's pure honesty and that's all anyone wants."

His blue eyes lit up. "You're absolutely right. Thanks, Brooke. I can't tell you how much I appreciate you talking to me."

"Any time." She hopped down from the rock. "I'd better get back. Big day tomorrow."

He stood too and nodded. "Oh, you know what? You just gave me a good in with Nick about coming to work for Garroway Paper."

Oh God. How could she have possibly done that?

"Well, I keep thinking how everything I have to offer Heather will work in my favor—stability, a great job, all that. And the same goes for you and Nick. There's clearly something between you two. And if he's going to take on twins, he'll need a real job, steady hours. Not some cowboy's life. He'll surely come work for us now. I just need to put it to him that way."

"Brandon," she said, putting a hand on his arm. "Trust me when I tell you that you will send him running for the hills with that approach. Besides, we're not even a couple."

The moment the words came out of her mouth the truth of it all stung like hell. Her heart clenched and her stomach flopped over.

"Well, any man who comes home to fulfill a promise to the jerk who saved his life and ends up as a nanny to twins is someone who will always do the right thing. That's what I need to appeal to. I'll get him."

If there were a contest for Most Frustrating Wyomingite, Brandon Garroway would take first place hands down. "But you shouldn't," she said—way more emotionally than she meant. "Nick has made his feelings clear. He wants to be a rancher. He doesn't want to work for Garroway Paper. Why can't you let him be who he is?"

"You just don't understand, Brooke. I thought that, as someone who took over her own family business, you would. But you just don't." He shook his head.

Oh, Brandon, it's you *who doesn't understand.* And boy, was he going to be in for a rude awakening. Someone had managed to capture his heart, and that someone was going to turn him upside down. She smiled at the thought. Brandon Garroway needed to be turned upside and shaken like a snow globe. Of course, there was no guarantee he'd change his tune.

There were no guarantees in life at all.

"I'm going to save my brother from throwing away his legacy. And I'm going to save Heather too."

Brooke gaped at him. "Save her? She may not be looking to be rescued in the slightest. A partner is one thing. But a real partner. Not someone who's looking to run her life. Brandon, you really need to think about these things."

He stood there, biting his lip, looking so unsure suddenly that she wanted to invite him back to the yurt for a glass of wine and a piece of pie. But the sanctuary was alcohol-free, and white flour was strictly forbidden. Somehow she didn't think the welcome bag of roasted chickpeas and green-tea soda water would do the trick.

And besides, Nick was in their yurt, and the last thing he needed right now was for his brother to be making more demands. At some point Nick was going to implode from the guilt it brought up. And things would be said, things she wasn't sure she'd want to hear, no matter who it had to do with.

Brandon was still shaking his head. "Brooke, you do you, and I'll do me." He put his hands in prayer formation and added, "Namaste," with a bow. Then he hurried off toward his yurt, which was two yurts down from hers and Nick's.

She would have rolled her eyes, but she felt for the guy. She really did. Love, in all its glory, was about to teach him some very important life lessons.

A croaking frog woke Nick up; the green-brown amphibian that was sitting on the other side of the window screen was making a racket. He might have laughed; he wasn't used to being woken up by frogs, but the realization that Brooke wasn't beside him took the smile off his face.

He found her note and glanced at the time on his phone on the bedside table. She'd been gone for almost an hour. The front door opened and he heard light footsteps, then the door close and lock. She was back.

And returning to his bed?

He waited, listening, but she never came in. He heard the gentle click of her door instead.

Disappointment flooded him. Did she need space? Time to think? Was she unsure what was going through his mind? He'd made it clear he was leaving town when her nanny returned in August, so perhaps she was focused on that.

Just go talk to her. Stop speculating. Stop her from speculating. Talk openly and honestly.

But he felt rooted to the bed. Mostly because he wasn't sure what he felt, what he'd say if he walked in her room.

He'd promised not to hurt her. He wasn't even sure if he could hurt her, or if he'd be the one getting his heart handed back to him. She'd told him she was done with love, that she couldn't trust right now. But then she'd realized she wanted the whole shebang. Love and marriage. A good father for her children. A life partner.

But still, maybe this was all too much, too soon.

Let's just see what happens. It's all we can do.

That was what they'd agreed to. So what was happening? With him and with her?

The frog croaked a bunch of times, and Nick looked out the window. Was he really going to lie here and not make sure Brooke was okay? That was the basis of his promise, wasn't it? *So get the hell up and go see.*

He slipped out of bed and left his room, giving her door a gentle knock so he wouldn't wake up the twins.

No response.

Knock again. And again, if you have to. If the twins wake up, they're your responsibility overnight anyway.

He knocked again.

He heard her footsteps coming to the door, and then there she was, beautiful Brooke.

"Are you trying to wake up the li'l screechers?" she asked with a smile, but he could see she was conflicted about something. Him, most likely.

"I was hoping you'd come back to my room," he said. "You were gone a while. What were you doing out there?"

"Sitting by the river, on the most beautiful flat-topped rock."

So, the frog had woken her up and she hadn't been able to go back to sleep, and so she'd gone for a walk and did some of that tree-staring or river-watching she'd mentioned was good for the soul and the mind.

"You okay?" he asked, reaching out a hand to her chin.

"I don't know. I don't know what's going on here. You're pulled in different directions. I've got a busy life. And we...slept together."

"You want to know what's going to happen," he said. A statement, not a question. Because he sure as hell couldn't answer it.

"Yeah. I want to know. And I know I can't possibly."

"So come back to my room. I'd come in here, but I don't want to be inappropriate in front of the youngins. Just come lie with me, Brooke. A warm body beside you is a hundred times more potent than looking at a tree or skipping stones in a river."

She grinned. "Is that a fact?"

"Yes. So come on." He peered past her at the twins, who were fast asleep. He held out his hand and held his breath for a second—but she took it.

They settled back in bed, him spooning her, his chin atop her head, one outstretched arm holding her hand. She curved into him perfectly.

He wanted to look at her, but he had a feeling she needed the space amidst the closeness. He sure did.

"I'm glad you came and got me," she said, holding his hand tighter.

"Me too," he whispered, and kissed the side of her face—half hair, half cheek.

For a while he lay there and listened to her breathe, their chests rising and falling in sync, and then he must have drifted off to sleep, because the next time he heard the frog croak, the sun was shining.

Chapter Eleven

The next day was such a whirlwind for Brooke that she barely had time to think about the incredible man she'd shared a bed with last night. No matter what happened between them, she'd never forget that he came for her. He could have let it go when he had heard her return from her walk and then go into her own room. He could have pretended to be asleep. Instead he knocked softly on her door until she opened it.

And then wrapped those strong arms around her, making her feel wanted and cherished and cared for. And she'd fallen right asleep.

In the morning she'd been grateful for the need to jump in the shower and get ready for the craziness that a wedding day always meant for the planner. Her complicated relationship with her manny was *not* on her very long do-now list, which filled three pages. She'd crossed off the entire first page as deliveries had come in, with Heather, the events manager and unexpected holder of Brandon Garroway's heart, working beside her to make sure all was accounted for.

Now, as she and Heather were alone in the open-air meditation hall, which had already been decorated for the reception with white chiffon and pink flowers threaded across the wooden beams of the structure, they pulled out the centerpieces and placed them on the tables. Today Heather's light blond hair was in two loose braids down both sides of her shoulders, almost reaching her waist. She wore another flowy outfit in a metallic silver, with a tree-of-life necklace and some silver bangles complementing it.

Heather was staring so hard at the one centerpiece she'd just placed on Table Four that Brooke knew she was deep in thought—about her own life and where love fit in. Brooke knew, because she'd done that kind of staring at many a wedding setup when she was pregnant.

Should she pipe up? She wanted to let Heather know she had a friend if she needed to talk, if she was scared, which Brooke was sure she was. But she didn't want to betray Brandon's confidence, and honestly Brooke wouldn't have necessarily appreciated someone coming at her with "been there, done that" advice. Sometimes she was grateful for advice, and sometimes it only scared her more and made her feel even more alone.

"Beautiful, aren't they," Brooke said, admiring the white-and-red roses in their short square tin vases that she set on Table Two.

Heather turned to her and bit her lip, slowly pulling out the last centerpiece. "Very. Just lovely. So, um, Brandon mentioned this morning that you might be a good person for me to know." Heather looked so unsure and nervous that Brooke wanted to give her a hug. "I'm only having one baby. I hear you have twins."

Brooke put her hand on Heather's arm. "It's scary regardless. Feeling alone is probably what caused the most stress. But my twins are the most wonderful thing that's ever happened to me."

Heather's entire face lit up. "That's how I feel. Scared but every time I think about having this baby in six months, I get ridiculously happy. Then scared, then happy." She laughed. "Is that how it's gonna go?"

Brooke smiled. "It has for me." She pulled a card out of her tote bag and handed it to Heather. "My cell phone is on there. Call me anytime, day or night, middle of the night, whenever. I'm completely serious. I wished I had someone to call when those scary thoughts gripped me or just when I had a question or wanted to talk through my thoughts."

"I really appreciate that." Heather glanced around as if to make sure a certain someone wasn't lurking nearby, then turned back to Brooke. "What do you think of Brandon? Kind of intense, huh?"

Brooke laughed. "That's a good word to describe him."

"And incredibly hot," Heather added. "Those blue eyes, my God."

"I'm in love with his brother," Brooke blurted out, then felt her eyes widen and she clamped a hand over her mouth. "Did I just say that out loud?"

Heather grinned. "Sorry, but yes."

Brooke couldn't help her own grin. "My *point* was

that the Garroway brothers look a lot alike, and yes, they're both very handsome."

"Love at first sight," Heather said, shaking her head with a smile. "A load of bunk."

Brooke walked around the tables to ensure all the centerpieces were indeed centered. "Not for Brandon."

Heather laughed, and then her smile faded. She picked up one of the centerpieces and brought it to her nose, inhaling. "No one's ever said half the stuff he said yesterday and this morning. I'm honestly afraid to believe any of it."

"I know what you mean. If I have any advice, it's to go with your gut, even if your head or heart are pulling you in different directions. Gut instincts rarely lie."

"My gut instincts tell me to give Brandon a chance. That he's just crazy enough to be very, very sane."

Brooke pulled Heather into a hug; she couldn't stop herself. "I'm glad to hear it."

"I just want to do everything right," Heather said. "It's not just me now."

"I know exactly what you mean. And you will. Just trust yourself."

Heather squeezed Brooke's hand, her hazel eyes much less troubled than earlier, then glanced toward the main lodge. "I hear the sound of a truck pulling in. Probably the caterer. And right on time."

The next couple of hours went by too fast as Brooke made sure everything was all set. A few little fires to put out, a momentary catastrophe when Cathy's daughter Lyndsey thought she'd left her dress at home—she hadn't—and then finally Brooke glanced down at her planner and checked her online calendar and crossed off the final thing on her list. She was done.

Now she had to get herself showered and dressed and be the behind-the-scenes person, which thankfully was also Heather's role. Brooke had worked with plenty of events managers who were so type A and high stress and nightmares to deal with that she was grateful to have this sweet, hardworking, creative dynamo as her partner today. Plus they had something else big in common besides this wedding: falling for Garroway men.

Back at the yurt, she found Nick sitting on the love seat with Mikey in his arms, feeding him a bottle. Her little baby boy, so beautiful—everything to her, along with his brother—was being cared for by this man she loved.

Loved. Loved. Loved. There was no way around the word. She loved Nick Garroway.

As if he heard her mind echoing, he turned and noticed her. "Hey. Sitter will be here in a minute to take the twins for a walk, and then she'll entertain them until bedtime. She's on duty till midnight. But I doubt we'll need her that long."

Brooke nodded. "The wedding starts at five, and we have the reception hall for five hours, so by the time I'm done making sure things that need to be returned are taken care of, I should be back by eleven, eleven thirty at the latest."

"Well, why don't you shower first while I finish feeding Mikey—Morgan already ate—and then I will."

Or we can shower together and stash the baby monitor on the little bookcase holding all the candles. The minute she'd seen the spa bath and all those candles, she'd imagined her and Nick in bubble heaven, with the lights turned low and some soft music.

Except the sitter might come early, as she had yesterday.

She smiled at Nick, grateful that he could not read her thoughts, and headed into her bedroom. A hot shower did wonders on her mind and stiff muscles. Within twenty minutes her hair was dry and twisted back into an elegant wedding chignon. She wore a pale blue sheath dress, nude heels, some light makeup and simple jewelry she'd inherited from her grandmother, including her beloved pin that read Dream Weddings on her chest.

"All set," she said as she came out of the bedroom.

Nick stood up, staring at her. "Wow. I've seen you dolled up but you look absolutely beautiful."

She grinned. "Why thank you, sir. I'm supposed to blend in, so I always dress like a guest when I work a wedding."

The Garroway blue eyes were intense on her. "You're stunning. I can't look away. Sorry."

That did seem to be the case. Could she melt in a puddle any more than she was already? How was it possible for one man to make her feel so special, so beautiful, so everything?

I love you, she wanted to yell. She could climb up to the top of the yurt and scream it for all to hear.

But Nick was walking past her, into his bedroom, giving her one last lingering look that sent tingles up her spine and goose bumps along her arms. He was remembering last night—and now she was too. Not that she'd forgotten. But all this busy day she'd forced herself not to think about being in bed with him.

Now it was all she could think about. And after the wedding…

"Ba ga!" Morgan shouted from his swing on the coffee table.

"Ga ga ba!" Mikey added, flinging his chew toy at his mama.

Ah, thank you for distracting me, boys, she thought, smiling at her sons. She eyed the burp cloth on the coffee table, reminding herself to use it if she went near one of the little imps.

Not long after Nick came out of his room, so unbelievably gorgeous and sexy in his "beach-fancy" tan suit sans the tie, the sitter arrived. And then he held out his arm and she wrapped her hand around it, and off they went. Like a couple.

But are we? she wondered, thinking back to what she'd said to Brandon. *We're not a couple.* Maybe they were. Or getting there.

Or maybe she was headed for heartbreak hotel.

"My dad and I weren't always close," Nick began, trying to keep his focus on his toast at his father's wedding and not on the forty pairs of eyes staring at him. He noticed his dad sit up straight at his words. Jeb was probably worried about where Nick was going with this speech. "But I think we're on our way."

He took another glance at Jeb Garroway and could plainly see the emotion in the man's eyes. And his new bride, Cathy, sitting right beside him, had tears shimmering in her own eyes.

"Nothing would make me happier—except maybe seeing how happy my father is because Cathy is in his life. The way the two of them interact makes me feel that anything is possible." He raised his glass of sparkling water—Cathy didn't drink alcohol and had requested a dry wedding. "So a toast and a thank-you to my father for making me believe that."

Everyone clapped and cheered, and the happy couple kissed. Cathy's daughters were up next, so he took his seat at the head table, between Brandon and Brooke.

"Beautiful and perfect," Brooke whispered.

"Nice job, brother," Brandon agreed, displaying warmth and approval in his gaze. A rarity coming from the guy. Nick would take it.

He waited for Brandon to start in on family unity and legacy, but his brother turned his attention to his appetizer of vegan dumplings with an array of sauces instead. *Definite progress here*, Nick thought, as relief flooded him. Maybe he and Brandon really could repair their relationship, be brothers again. That would mean the world to Nick.

He forked a dumpling and dipped it into a sweet-and-sour sauce before popping it in his mouth. Delicious. "I like this wedding," he said to Brooke, realizing it had a lot to with her.

She grinned. "Thanks. Everything has gone off without a hitch. Ahh, so nice to sit back and relax for a few moments."

Jeb Garroway stood and tapped a fork against his glass. "I'd like to make a toast now."

The meditation hall quieted, not that it was all that loud before. All eyes turned to Nick's father.

"I loved listening to my sons' speeches," Jeb began. "To have both my sons with me today means everything to me. And I know Cathy feels that way about having her daughters here. We're starting a new life and you four are starting it with us. I know that someday soon the four of you will find partners to share your life with who will bring the joy and happiness that Cathy has brought to my life. Nothing else will ever be as important as love and family."

There were cheers and clapping, and a wolf whistle from Brandon. But then Nick noticed his brother's eyes had shifted over to a tree outside the meditation hall, where a young woman who worked for the sanctuary stood, watching. Heather, Nick thought her name was. She had a wistful expression on her face, and as Nick glanced at Brandon, who was staring at her, he realized his brother had it bad for the woman. He wasn't quite sure he'd ever seen that expression on Brandon's face.

"Something going on between those two?" Nick whispered into Brooke's ear, with a wag of his finger between Brandon and the tree just beyond the opening to the hall.

Brooke smiled. "Yup."

"Well, love is certainly in the air," he said, stiffening the moment the word *love* had tumbled out of his mouth. *Because we're at a wedding*, he wanted to rush to add. Amend. Correct.

"Is it?" she whispered, leaning closer, with a breathtaking smile and her beautiful driftwood-brown eyes now staring into his.

He froze like the ole deer in headlights, and because he was so obviously uncomfortable by the question, she glanced away, her cheeks slightly flushed, and picked up her drink. She took a long sip and then made small talk with Brandon about the dumplings.

Oh no. He'd screwed up. Hard and fast. It was a good thing he hadn't been eating one of those dumplings when asked the very simple question he'd brought up in the first place, because he would have choked and someone would have had to come over to give him the Heimlich.

Why did you have to bring up love if you can't handle talking about it? Idiot, he yelled at himself.

And there was no easy way to fix things between them right now without saying a bunch of stuff that would make it all worse and more awkward. He'd been there.

"Well, I'm going to see how the entrées are coming," Brooke said, rushing off her chair and out of the meditation tent toward the main lodge, where the facility kitchen was.

"Go after her," Brandon whispered. "Make things right."

Nick whirled around and faced his brother. "Eavesdropper."

"Hey, you guys are sitting two inches from me. You're just going to let her run off? Unless a lady tells you specifically not to follow, you follow and make it right. Say whatever you need to to fix things."

Nick scowled. "Whatever I need to? What if I don't know what the hell I want to say?"

"Well, that's your problem, isn't it," Brandon said. "Figure it out."

Luckily some friends of Cathy's came over to their table just then to compliment the brothers on their speeches, so Nick was saved from more talk with his brother about his love life. This was certainly a first.

In a way it was kind of nice. But Nick wasn't used to talking about his...feelings with anyone.

"Go," Brandon ordered as the group moved on.

"Yes, sir," Nick said, standing up and pushing in his chair. He turned to go, then looked at his brother. "Oh, and Brandon?"

"Yeah?" his brother asked, dipping another dumpling into a ginger sauce.

"Thanks," Nick said.

Brandon gave him something of a smile and a nod, which told Nick that that the guy was moved. For a second he could see fourteen-year-old Brandon in his brother's face, before their mother died, before, before, before, and it was like he had his kid brother back. It had been a long time since Nick had done anything that warmed the heart of Brandon Garroway. And now he'd done it twice in the last hour. It felt good.

And the only thing that could top this feeling was to find Brooke and make things right between them. Somehow.

Brooke was counting saffron-risotto-primavera entrées when she saw Nick enter the kitchen. She wanted to duck down and hide, but she was a grown-up. "Thirty-eight, thirty-nine," she said, nodding at the waitstaff. "Okay, guys, you can take these beauties out, and thank you."

As the three waiters filled up their huge trays, Nick stepped closer.

"Wow, that smells good," he said. "And *looks* good. I don't think I've ever had vegan food."

"Well, you have, without thinking about it. Potato chips are vegan."

"Ah. I do like chips," he said, making it clear how much easier it must be for him to talk food than feelings. He stared at her, then reached for her hand. "And I like *you*, Brooke." His face flushed in a way she'd never seen before. "I mean, of course I like you. Duh," he added, his voice getting very pitchy. "Oh God, I am making a colossal mess out of this."

Her heart clenched and her stomach twisted. All symptoms of a little something called heartache. She'd had that malady before. "Nick, let me put you out of your misery. I'm the one who said damn the torpedoes. *Que sera, sera*, I'd basically said, right? So no worries. I'm a big girl. I got caught up in the heat of the moment last night, and then all the romance at the wedding. Forget it, okay?" She forced a smile on her face that she hoped looked natural. *Yeah, sure it does.*

He stood there, staring at her, clearly wanting to say something but unable to articulate it.

He doesn't love you. That's the thing. He'd probably like to, but he doesn't. And Nick Garroway is not a liar.

Her eyes stung and she blinked back at it hard. "I need to check the tables, make sure the waiters are clearing appetizer plates properly," she said, and rushed out into the fresh, clean air, which she gulped down.

Do not cry, she told herself. *Your mascara will run and you'll look like a sad raccoon.*

But tears misted her eyes anyway.

How could this be over before it had even really started?

Chapter Twelve

That went well. *Not.* Nick kept looking for Brooke throughout the rest of the wedding, to talk to her—to try to anyway—but she'd made herself scarce. Every now and then he'd spot her in huddles with Sanctuary staff or Heather, whom he now noticed was dancing cheek to cheek with Brandon to a jazz standard.

He looked at the time on his phone. Just a few minutes to ten. The wedding was over, and the guests would be heading to their cars, save the few who'd booked yurts. Tomorrow he'd be back at Brooke's—

He hadn't really considered that. He was her manny till August, and he had to make things right between them. He had to be there for her, no matter what their status was. That promise he'd never go back on.

He caught Brooke giving final directions to two of

Heather's event staff about packing up the wedding gear, and then she headed over to the dance floor, where his father and Cathy were swaying, both looking very happy. She hugged each of them, and then he watched her leave the meditation hall, slip off her heels and head toward the river.

Right behind you, he thought. He let his father and Cathy know he was heading out, congratulated them again, wished them a great honeymoon if he didn't see them in the morning and then hurried after Brooke.

She was sitting on a flat-topped rock, throwing pebbles into the water.

"Can I sit here?" he asked, looking at the space beside her.

She started, clearly surprised to see him there, and gave a half shrug.

He took that as a yes and hopped up, glancing at the collection of pebbles she'd put beside her. "I've got *a lot* on my mind, Brooke. It feels like a jumble—that's the best way I can describe it. All I know for sure is that I want to be with you and the twins. I want to take care of the three of you."

She glanced at him, then back at the river, whooshing along the plants and rocks. "I know. But I'm looking for a husband, and a father for Mikey and Morgan. That's what I want. That's what I need. A life partner. Not a rescuer. Not a promise-fulfiller. Someone who's there because he wants to be. Every day."

A lump grew in his throat. A husband. A father. Was that him? Why did his head feel like it was stuffed with steel wool?

"I know what I want," she added. "You don't." She

stared at the water and her expression was so sad that he wanted to gather her in his arms and just hold her, tell her everything would be okay.

But of course he couldn't. He'd lost that ability, and it made him feel like hell.

Her expression changed—resolute, chin lifted. "And look, Nick, I can handle the twins from here on. My nanny is due back next week. I can take care of Morgan and Mikey, and do what I need to on the Satler wedding, on my own for a week. No problem there."

But...

Wait.

So, she was saying he wasn't her manny anymore? This was it? Didn't he just tell her he wanted to be with the Timber family, to take care of them? That was what he wanted.

And hadn't she just said what *she* wanted? A life partner. Not a rescuer.

Oh hell.

She hopped off the rock and picked up her heels. "I'm exhausted. Since this is your last night on duty, I wouldn't mind if you kept the twins with you in your room overnight. I could really use a solid night's sleep."

"Of course," he said, feeling his chest squeezing.

His final night with the twins. And Brooke—in the next room anyway. So, tomorrow morning they'd drive back to her house and he'd pack his duffel bag and leave?

That was exactly what he'd do. He'd go buy that ranch he'd been dreaming of for months.

That was his future. Him and the ranch, a couple of

horses, the cattle, sheep, and chickens, and a few rescue dogs.

Alone and without Brooke or her boys.

That was what he wanted?

Nick's entire life was in a green duffel bag and one
garment bag containing his tan suit. How was that possible? This was everything he owned? He scowled at
the realization that he didn't have much to his name,
except a decent bank account.

It had taken him five seconds to pack, and he'd been
hoping to prolong it. He and Brooke had barely spoken
on the two-hour ride back to Wedlock Creek. He'd had
so much to say and nothing at all. And now here was,
standing in the guest room of Brooke's house, ready
to go.

Dammit.

He slung the duffel over his shoulder and draped
the garment bag over his arm. He'd said goodbye to
the twins already. He'd actually said his goodbyes last
night, in the yurt, and the fact that his eyes stung while
doing so hadn't escaped him.

He loved those babies.

But he'd done what he'd come to do, he supposed,
and then his relationship with Brooke had taken on a
life of its own, and now it was time to go. She wasn't
okay, because of him—and that was against the rules.
But this was one time where he couldn't fix things. Not
the way she needed them fixed.

When they'd gotten back this morning, she'd asked
if he'd stay with the twins for a half hour while she
did some grocery shopping, and he'd been grateful for

the extra time with the boys. But then they'd gotten tired and he'd put them down for their naps, standing there over their cribs and staring at them. He'd gotten all...*verklempt* watching them sleep, their little bow mouths quirking. *This can't be it*, he'd thought, shaking his head. At the situation, at himself.

He'd been beside himself, so he'd given the house a final quick cleaning. He'd cleaned Snowball and Smudge's food and water bowls, changed the cat litter, his least favorite task, and scratched their backs the way they liked. He'd miss the independent fur balls. He'd also done the twins' laundry, and as he'd tossed a bunch of burp cloths in for a white wash, his heart seized. A tiny white square of cloth shouldn't have such an effect on a former soldier, but it did. And he hadn't been thinking about Elena or Aisha. He hadn't been thinking about his mother or the years he'd spent Thanksgiving and Christmas without family.

He'd only thought about Brooke and the twins.

He heard her key in the lock and came downstairs. She opened the door and her gaze landed on it, and he saw her suck in a breath at the sight of him—and his luggage.

She gave him a bit of a smile and walked in, holding up the grocery bag. "I bought three blocks of cheese, and I'll be having a roast-beef sandwich for lunch, with a bottle of my favorite Wyoming beer. A weekend is too long to go without cheese and alcohol."

He appreciated her trying to lighten things. "I hear ya. I wonder if my dad will be giving up his nightly bourbon, since Cathy doesn't drink. Name of love, I guess."

He froze again, and her cheeks flushed. What the

hell was wrong with him? Had he just done it again? He had. He really had.

He shook his head at himself. "I'm really, really bad at this. If it wasn't clear before, it is now."

She looked at him, her expression going from sad to forced neutral. "I guess we're all just who we are, right? Can't try to be something we're not."

He swallowed. He wished he could be. Because this sure as hell didn't feel like him.

"Need help putting anything away?" he asked, gesturing at the grocery bag.

"Nah. Thanks for everything." She turned her back to him and he knew she was crying.

Oh hell.

"The twins are napping," he said. "If you need anything, Brooke, you just call me. Text me. I'll be here in two seconds. Anytime, day or night."

She nodded, her back still turned to him.

"I guess this is goodbye," he said.

She turned around and lifted her chin. "I guess it is."

He took one last look at her, and Snowball and Smudge weaved in between his legs one last time, as though they *knew*. Then he hoisted his duffel and left before he imploded.

Nick didn't want to stay at his father's house without his permission—and wasn't about to text him on his honeymoon—and he wasn't quite ready to even ask Brandon about staying at his condo, so he got a room at the Wedlock Creek Inn. The bed-and-breakfast was just a minute's drive from Brooke's, at the far end of Main Street. If she did need him, he could be there in a flash.

He tossed the duffel onto the bed. The room was nice enough—*too* nice, since he missed the simplicity of the yurt in a really-missing-Brooke-and-the-twins way. He sat down and pulled out his phone, checking the notes he'd made on the ranches for sale. Going to check them out would distract him, give him something to do. A few were a couple of hours away, but he didn't like the idea of being that far away if Brooke needed him. An emergency. Anything. He should stay reasonably local, just in case.

There were two ranches for sale within twenty minutes, one just ten minutes out. He'd go see that one. He called the owner to set something up and got lucky—the guy was free in an hour. That would give him time to lie down and come to grips with what had happened, where he was, where he *wasn't*, and clear his head.

Ping. A text. He grabbed his phone, hoping it was Brooke, hoping she needed something heavy moved or a screen door fixed, but it was Brandon.

It was crazy how his chest squeezed at the sight of Brandon's name on his phone—probably same as it would have if it *had* been Brooke. Until very recently he hadn't had a text from his brother in twelve years. Now suddenly they had a relationship.

Lunch at 1:00 p.m.? Have a crazy update about Heather—the woman of my dreams—if you're interested.

Nick grinned. *Well, I'll be,* he drawled to himself, wishing he had a cowboy hat to take off like John Wayne would have in surprised respect. His brother wanted to talk about his love life—with Nick. Nick texted back.

Meet you at Burger Heaven?

See you then.

And perfect timing. He was meeting a Henry Fieldstone at the ranch for sale, at eleven o'clock, and would be back in town by twelve forty-five at the latest.

He unpacked his few things to remind him that this was home for the time being, and then did some research on the ranch he'd be checking out. Right size, but a lot closer than he'd ever intended to be to Wedlock Creek. Then again, with things so good between him and his family, maybe he should consider staying within thirty minutes.

He left the inn, grabbed an iced coffee from Java Jane's in the hopes that Brooke might be in there with the twins, just so he could see her again, but she wasn't, and then drove the half hour to the Three Dog Ranch.

He liked the name, and the owner even had a big iron sign above the gate, with the silhouette of three dogs. The half-mile drive from the road to the ranch house was lined with huge trees, and the moment the house came into view, the three dogs bounded up to the car, running alongside till he parked it. He gave the three happy-looking mutts a pat, then extended his hand to Henry, a man in his midsixties, wearing a Stetson, jeans and work boots. He had some hay stuck to the side of his jeans, and Nick thought he'd like to have that problem.

"Love that smell of this country air," Nick said.

"Me too. But I promised my wife we'd retire to Southern California, where it's always warm, so I'm looking to sell. I love this place, but it's time to go."

He understood that sentiment all too well. "Well, if I bought the place, I'd keep the name and the sign, since I'm planning on adopting a couple of dogs myself. I'll have to get three, of course."

Henry laughed and began showing him around. The white farmhouse was in nice condition; it had a big gray barn that had a huge weather vane atop it, and almost fifteen hundred acres. He'd had a lot more cattle than he did now, but he'd sold most in preparation for the big move. A creek ran a thousand feet behind the house, and a chicken coop, painted hot pink, was already beside the barn.

"Wife loves pink," Henry said. "The chickens were her pet project. The coop and chickens would stay."

He wondered if Brooke would like ranch life. He tried to imagine her chatting up a hen as they collected eggs together on an ordinary morning. What was he doing? Why was he even thinking about it? He'd never intended to get married. To anyone.

But he could see Brooke sitting on the porch with her notes and planning a wedding, along with the Timber twins running around the yard, playing with the dogs. There was a gorgeous screened-in porch on the back side of the house, facing a well-tended garden, with sliding glass doors to a patio. He could see it as the Dream Weddings office.

He swallowed. He could see it. He could see it all.

Brooke here. Children running around. A family, a life. Love. Commitment. Forever. The present and future in one.

But did he actually want it to happen? Why was he so damned stuck?

And besides, Brooke had a nice house, with her home office, and why would she want to move ten minutes out to the country, away from town and clients and her vendors?

Stop thinking about it.

An hour later he'd toured the property with Henry in his open Jeep, and listened as Henry told him the history of the place and the livestock he'd had, how the ranch had operated full swing. Nick drank it all in intently; he did want this life. Badly. He wanted to live here.

Then it was time to go. He shook Henry Fieldstone's hand again, thanked him for the tour and information, and said he was very interested and would be in touch. He gave the dogs a last pat, took another look around and felt himself relax at the thought of this being his home. He then got in his truck and headed back to town.

He wished he could talk to Brandon about the ranch, get his opinion from a financial perspective, since his brother was a businessman and money guy, but he had no doubt Brandon would be upset that he was really planning on becoming a rancher instead of a paper pusher—literally—at Garroway Paper.

Maybe he'd keep the conversation to the women in their lives instead. Not that talking about Brooke would be any less difficult.

* * *

Brooke should have been working on the Satler wedding, but she couldn't focus, not today. And with her heart barely hanging on, the last thing she wanted to do was to plan someone else's big day.

She pushed the stroller up the path in Wedlock Creek Park, turning onto the grass and heading for the stately oak tree, where the boys' favorite nature show, *The Lenny and Squiggy Race*, was always playing. She spread out a big blanket, parked the stroller and sat down beside it, waiting for the squirrels to make their appearance.

"I don't see Lenny and Squiggy, but I'll bet they're around here somewhere," she said.

"Ba da ga," Mikey said, shaking his stuffed lion in his hand with a big gummy smile.

"Ta ba," Morgan agreed, banging his fists on the little tray in front of his seat.

"Ah, there's one squirrel," she said, but it was too small and skinny to be either Lenny or Squiggy. Still, the furry gray creature darted from one branch to another, coming even closer as it surveyed the scene, then squeaked and started eating an acorn.

"Ba ba da!" Mikey said, mesmerized by the quick moving actions.

She'd never gotten to show Nick the park. Or the squirrels. She wondered what he was doing right now. Where he was staying. Maybe at his father's. Or his brother's. She couldn't quite see either.

What she would give to go home and find him in the kitchen, unloading the dishwasher or making spaghetti with his excellent meat sauce or folding the twins' onesies. Or just to find him sitting on the sofa, doing absolutely nothing but being a great guy—just one who didn't love her.

She held back the sob that threatened. Be present for the twins, she reminded herself, her gaze on her children. You can't let a broken heart send you into a tailspin. They need you. You need you. The Satler sisters need you.

But she could use a good cry. She'd had one last night. Since Nick had kept the twins in his room at the yurt, she'd let herself cry long and hard over him, her hand stifling her sobs so he wouldn't hear and burst in and insist on holding her. Could you make someone feel better if you were the cause of their heartbreak?

She couldn't blame him anyway. She'd caused her own pain. She knew what she was getting into and she leaped right in anyway. She could hear her grandmother quoting, *Better to have loved and lost than never to have loved at all. No matter how bad it hurts.*

Brooke agreed. But it did hurt.

Nick took a bite of his maple-bacon barbecue burger. Ah, that was good. He could barely believe he was sitting in Burger Heaven with his brother. They used to come here a lot, years ago. Many years ago. The owners had changed a couple of times, but the burgers were still amazing, and the fries perfect.

He'd never forget taking Brandon here in the days after their mother was diagnosed. Brandon had been a wreck, feeling sure they were going to lose her. Nick had been a wreck too, but he'd wanted to be strong for his brother. Maybe he'd been too strong—outwardly. Maybe he'd made Brandon think he wasn't as affected as he was. But they'd come here and sat in the booth second from the door on the left, ordered two cheeseburgers with the works, and then both had just sat, staring at their plates, unable to touch their food, with Brandon sobbing. Nick had gone over to his side of the booth and put his arm around him, and the waitress had left him alone, except to bring a box of tissues, which Nick had appreciated. That waitress was still here too. He'd made a point of sitting in her section, unsure if she'd even remember them, but he wanted to be able to leave her a big tip.

"So, last night, after the wedding," Brandon said, "Heather and I met at the riverbank and sat there, talking for hours. We didn't leave until well after 2:00 a.m. And when I got back to my yodi or whatever that tent cabin is called, I lay in my bed, staring at the circular ceiling for hours, freaked out of my mind."

Nick smiled. "It's called a yurt. And if you and Heather are a couple, you should learn the lingo."

"We *are* a couple."

"Yurt. Yurt, yurt, yurt."

"Ha, ha," Brandon said, narrowing his eyes and taking a bite of his burger. But he grinned. "So, the thing I'm freaked out about is something you could probably help me with."

Nick couldn't be more surprised. "What's that?"

"How'd you learn how to be a manny?" Brandon asked. "You seemed to know what you were doing immediately, even that first or second day at the dinner at Dad's house. How'd you know how to even hold a baby or what to do when?"

That was when Brandon filled him in on Heather's pregnancy. *Wow*, Nick thought. Brandon really was full of surprises.

Nick smiled and thought of Aisha. It was crazy how those memories didn't poke and sting anymore. They simply felt like good memories. Right before he'd left Texas, he'd called the orphanage where Elena worked in Afghanistan and had asked how she was, how the adoption was going, and he'd been assured the two were doing great and that Elena was planning on bringing the baby home to Indiana by the end of summer.

"Turns out all you have to do is hold a baby once," Nick said, "and you kind of figure it out as you go." It was the truth. That was how he'd comforted Aisha in that first crazy hour he'd found her. And then he'd done some quick research on what a baby needed, based on her age, and he'd acted accordingly.

"Maybe I can practice with Brooke's twins," Brandon suggested. "Or twin. I'd like to stick with one."

Nick laughed. "I'm sure she'd loan you one for an hour or so in her house. It's like anything else new. You learn as you go. The key, though, is caring. That's half the battle, really."

Brandon took a sip of his beer. "Caring? What do you mean?"

"Well, when you care, really care, about something or someone, you want to get it right, you know?"

"I hope I get this thing with Heather right," Brandon said, frowning. "I know I can be a bit much. That's what my admin tells me sometimes anyway. It's why I haven't fired her for her insubordination. She calls me out when I need it."

Who knew there were so many sides to Brandon Garroway? Not Nick, that was for sure. He certainly hadn't known his brother appreciated pushback. There'd been a lot of that between them, particularly recently.

"I've been thinking about your refusal to come work for Garroway Paper," Brandon said.

Nick felt his appetite slip away. Good thing he'd eaten most of his burger already. "And?"

"I think what I need to do with the baby I'll be raising is start him or her in the business early. From the get-go. Bring the baby to work, even as an infant, talk about my day in the office and what I'm doing while I'm doing it. Kind of the way people talk to babies anyway. Isn't that how babies learn to speak?"

Nick could hear the tot's first word already: *paper.*

"Dad didn't do that," Brandon continued. "With either of us. But luckily I had it in my blood and veins anyway, so all's good. But for someone like you, who doesn't have that gene where family legacy is important, it needs to be instilled from birth. Every day."

...who doesn't have that gene where family legacy is important...

"I never said Garroway Paper wasn't important to me," Nick snapped, hating that his back was up.

"You didn't have to. The company *isn't* important to you. But I know now how to make sure it is important to my son or daughter."

Deep sigh.

Nick had been hoping that, with Brandon falling in love and putting someone else first, his brother might start to see the world and his piece of it differently. Nope.

"And what if this child you raise doesn't want to work at Garroway Paper, Brandon?"

"I can't see how that would happen if the baby grows up in the office, learning about paper from infancy. We'll spend all the major development periods in all the departments. Trust me, my child will have a love of paper and the family business."

Sure sounded like a lot to heap on a child who wasn't even born yet. "And if even after raising your kid at Garroway Paper, he or she wants to go a different path? Then what? Disowned? Out of the family? Out of the will? You go from love to indifference and disappointment just like that?"

Brandon looked away, chewing the inside of his mouth, and Nick could tell he'd finally gotten through that thick skull, even just a tiny crack. "Well, I'd be disappointed, yeah."

Nick let out a breath. His brother just didn't get it, and now Nick had gotten it through his own thick skull that he just had to let it go. The two of them were never going to see eye to eye on this. And that had to be okay. Because there was no other way for them to be brothers, to have a relationship.

"Can we agree to disagree on the subject?" Nick asked.

Brandon shrugged. "The company needs you. We'll be here when you get this ranching thing out of your system. Because that's how family is supposed to work.

I was mad at you for a long time, Nick. But I shouldn't have tried to kick you out of the family. That was wrong. When you're ready to join Garroway Paper, we'll be here for you."

Nick swallowed. The apology, if that was what it was, meant a lot to Nick. But he was never going to work at the company. Never. And he was tired of saying so. The good news was they'd reached their truce, a place where they could move on.

"Okay, then," Nick said, extending his hand.

Brandon shook it. "I never did get your advice about Heather. Here's my question. Would you propose right now or wait? She thinks we should wait till we know each other better, but I know what I need to know *now*. I want to marry her. I want to legally adopt the baby the moment he or she is born."

"Wow, you really love this woman," Nick said in total wonder.

"When you know, you know. And if I'm nuts and this blows up in my face, at least I tried. At least I went with my gut. Right?"

At least I tried. Nick hadn't tried very hard with Brooke, had he? Because his gut was sending him in the opposite direction. To the Three Dog Ranch. Alone.

"Follow your gut," Nick agreed. "Propose. It'll be up to her to accept or not. Worst'll happen is that you'll propose again in a couple of months."

Brandon beamed. "I already bought a ring. One carat. That'll show her I'm dead serious." He reached into his jacket pocket and pulled out a velvet ring box and opened it. The diamond was huge and twinkled. Wow. Good for Brandon.

"I hope she says yes," Nick said, wishing he had it in him to propose to Brooke.

But right now he couldn't imagine doing so. And he wasn't sure why.

Chapter Thirteen

As a wedding planner, Brooke thought she'd heard it all. She'd gotten her share of out-there requests. The groom who thought it would be "fun" if his four prior girlfriends were invited to the reception, only in order to watch the first dance and see what they had lost out on. The bride who'd met her groom at a fast-food restaurant and wanted to "pipe in the particular aroma of those yummy burgers and fries" during the ceremony. Brooke had talked both out of those. Then there was the mother of the bride who thought Brooke's role included babysitting all children at the wedding. No.

At this point she figured nothing anyone asked, for any reason, wedding or otherwise, could surprise her. Until she got a call yesterday from Brandon Garroway, asking if he could be a "mother's helper" for a couple of hours to learn the ropes of taking care of a baby. "I need to show Heather I'm serious," he'd said. "You can vouch for me that I basically took a class by training with you."

Between being heartbroken and busy with the Satler wedding, and managing without her excellent manny, Brooke had wanted to say that she just didn't have time to "train" a complete newbie in the art of baby care. But he'd been so danged earnest and she had to admit she'd been a bit moved by how hard he was trying.

He *was* trying. Other men with the last name *Garroway* weren't trying at all.

So now Brandon was in her living room, bent over the stroller, watching her every movement and taking notes. He'd brought a small notebook with him and had filled three pages already. When Brandon had first arrived, he'd asked why the babies were "just sitting there" and if that was normal. So she'd spent fifteen minutes on development and stages, and he'd stood there in wide-eyed wonder, scrawling away in his notebook.

"And that's how you unlatch the five-point harness," she said, doing exactly that. "Then you reach in, scoop up the baby, careful to protect the neck if an infant, like so, and voilà, you're holding a baby."

Brandon nodded. "Got it. Can you put Mikey back in and latch him up? I want to start from scratch."

She smiled, mentally shaking her head. "This is Morgan, but yes."

For the next hour, Brandon played house, and Brooke had to say that he really seemed to be enjoying himself. He'd watched how she fed Mikey and then carefully positioned Morgan for his bottle, careful to hold the bottle just so, and when Mikey let out a satisfying burp, Brandon looked like he'd won a spectacular prize. He'd played with both twins in their swings and then ran up to the nursery to choose storybooks to read them. And finally he practiced packing the stroller bag and then placing a baby in the stroller.

"Extra diapers, pack of wipes, burp cloths, change of pj's, sun hat, baby sunscreen—check," he said with an accomplished smile, recalling the necessities for a summer stroll out on Main Street.

"You really want this to work with Heather, huh?" Brooke asked. She was truly touched by his passion. She had no idea if it could be lasting, if once Brandon actually got to know Heather, lovely as she seemed, they'd have any real chemistry or get along or have anything in common, for that matter, but for now he was in the throes of a fantasy and she hoped it did work out. Stranger things had happened.

"Yes, I do. She's special. And the one. I've always heard I'd know it when I found her. And crazy as it is, since we just met a week ago, I *know.* I knew from the minute I laid eyes on her. Like you and Nick. You guys just knew."

There went her eyes again, stinging away. "Nick was my nanny. That's all. We were never a couple."

It had been a full week since they'd returned from Sagebrush Sanctuary and Retreat, and though she hadn't seen him since, Nick had texted every day with the same message. Just checking in.

And she'd text back.

Everything's fine. No need to ask. I'll let you know if the sky falls.

He'd send back a smiley-face emoji, but the next day he sent the same text. Just checking in.

A week without laying eyes on his face, hearing his voice. It was hell.

"Oh, please," Brandon said. "You so are a couple. He's being stubborn, right?"

"How'd you know?" she asked before she could stop herself. She shouldn't be talking about Nick behind his back—and not with Brandon. Nick would *not* like that.

"I know. Same way I know he belongs at Garroway Paper and not some ranch, chasing cows around a pasture. He's being stubborn about that and he's being stubborn about his real feelings for you. He can't face it. He can't face any of it."

Was it wrong that she was very interested in his brother's psychoanalysis? That very subject was all Brooke could think about last night and today. Why this and why that, and if only this and if only that.

"I know he'll come around to working for the company," Brandon said. "And trust me, the way he is with you? The way he looks at you? He's in love and has no idea."

She bit her lip, hoping against hope that Brandon was right. But she didn't want him to be right about Garroway Paper, since she knew that wasn't the case. Nick wanted to be a rancher. Not working in an office, even if it was the family business.

So, was it dopey to hope he was right about the second part—the part where she came in?

Brandon's phone rang and he glanced at it. "It's Cathy," he said with a smile. "They probably just got back from London." He clicked a button. "Hey, Cathy, how was the honeymoon?" He listened, his smile turning into a frown, then a grimace, and then his hands started shaking.

"Brandon, what is it?" Brooke asked, panic rising.

"My dad collapsed at the airport. He was rushed to Brewer General, twenty minutes away."

Oh no. "Did Cathy call Nick?" she asked.

He nodded but looked like he might faint. He was just standing there, trembling, still holding the phone in his hand.

She quickly put Morgan in the stroller, beside Mikey. "I'll drive. Let's go," she said, throwing open the door and rushing to her car. She got the boys in their car seats and hurried to the driver's side, but Brandon was standing by the car door, his complexion ashen. She ran around and opened the door and guided him in. "Hey, let's get over to the hospital," she said, giving his hand a squeeze before shutting the door and running back around to the driver's side.

As she drove, Brandon's cell rang and he answered it. "We're on our way," he said, his voice cracking. "Did you hear anything? Is he okay?" He listened, biting his lip, and Brooke's heart broke for how nervous and scared he was. "Okay. Okay. See you soon."

"Was that Nick?" she asked. "They're doing tests?"

He nodded. "They don't know what's wrong yet. Cathy is beside herself."

"We'll be there in ten minutes," she assured him, driving as fast as she could without risking anyone's life or getting pulled over. Finally they arrived at the Emergency entrance, and against all odds someone was pulling out of a prime spot just as they were coming in. She grabbed the spot and got the twins into the stroller in record time, and they rushed in.

Nick stood at the sight of them. He looked as stricken as his brother, his face so pale, the blue eyes worried and scared.

Brandon flew into Cathy's arms for a hug. "Have you heard anything?" Brandon asked.

"An ER doctor came out to talk to us just a few minutes ago," Cathy said. "She said Jeb had a minor heart attack."

"What?" Brandon choked out. He stared from Cathy to Nick and back to Cathy.

Cathy took Brandon's hands. "He's going to be fine. It was minor. But it means he needs to take a couple of weeks off and take it very easy and change his diet. I've been after him about that, but trust me, he'll be eating the Cathy way from now on."

"He's going to be okay?" Brandon sank into a chair, staring from Cathy to Nick.

Nick nodded. "The doctor said Dad appears to be out of the woods and indications are that he should make a full recovery." Regardless, he looked so shaken and upset that Brooke wished she could pull him into an embrace, soothe him somehow. But of course she couldn't. "He'll take medication and, as Cathy said, completely relax for a couple of weeks. We can go see him in about ten minutes. A nurse will come get us."

Brandon sucked in a breath and let it out. "Okay. He's going to be fine. We've got a big meeting this week that

Dad was looking forward to, but I'll handle it. And I won't send him any details. No work, no news of work. He should just relax."

Cathy nodded. "We're on the same page, then. No talk of work or the office. Not a peep."

Brandon nodded. "I've got this, Dad," he whispered to no one in particular, then squeezed his eyes shut.

Nick stood up. "I won't leave you in the lurch, Brandon. You or Dad. And you too, Cathy. You're part of this family now. So I'll be joining Garroway Paper."

Brandon's eyes popped open and he gasped. "Really?"

Really? Brooke wanted to second but Nick looked as serious as a... She sighed, thinking he was operating on the same thoughts that had him becoming her manny. Doing what he thought was right. Regardless of what he wanted or needed. But that was Nick Garroway.

Nick nodded, standing ramrod straight, like a soldier. "Tomorrow's Monday. Good day to start."

Brandon stood up and extended his hand, then pulled Nick into a brief hug. "Means a lot, Nick. Thanks."

Nick nodded, and Brooke tried to read his expression. Somewhere between determined and grim.

Cathy patted Nick on the shoulder, and Brooke sent him a smile, but she couldn't keep it on her face.

Was Nick really going to work for Garroway Paper? He was going to show up tomorrow, at 9:00 a.m., in a suit and tie, with a briefcase, and become passionate about paper? Okay, his reasons for joining the family business had nothing to do with paper and everything to do with his dad, who was lying on a hospital cot. And about his brother, who needed him.

Finally a nurse came in and said they could go see the patient, two at a time. Nick sent Brandon and Cathy, and he and Brooke sat back down, Brooke giving the stroller a gentle push as Mikey started to fuss a bit.

"You're joining Garroway Paper temporarily until your dad is back on his feet?" she asked.

"I'm not looking at it that way," he said, his blue eyes full of emotions she couldn't pinpoint. Regret and resolve, maybe. Worry. Sadness. "I'm needed there. My dad needs me. My brother needs me. That's all that matters. We could have lost my father. Just like that—gone. Like my mother. I want to do what's right."

Oh, Nick, she thought. But she couldn't say anything, so she just reached out for his hand and held it.

On Monday Nick put on the tan suit and showed up for work at Garroway Paper an hour early, at 8:00 a.m. He'd barely slept last night, his mind a jumble—the company, his dad's health, the fear in his brother's eyes, even though Jeb was okay. And Brooke. Seeing her last night at the hospital with the twins had seemed so natural, as though of course she'd been there, because she was family.

He hadn't blinked an eye at her being there. Until he'd realized why. And then his skin had gotten all itchy. The word *family* was loaded for him—maybe that was why. He'd tossed and turned, trying to figure it all out, and then he'd given up and read over some Garroway Paper information he'd asked Brandon to email him. The reports might as well have been in French or Swahili for all he could make sense of them. And they were boring as hell too.

He was sure he'd find his niche in the company. He'd try a few departments and see where he might be able to do some good. There had to be one. He wasn't a business guy. Or a finance guy. Or a salesman. He was all right at strategy though, making a plan and leading troops through dangerous territory. There might be some kind of equivalence at Garroway Paper, sort of.

There was one car in the parking lot when he arrived. Brandon's. He parked beside him and headed in, sucking in a deep breath as he pulled open the glass door.

Here goes nothing. And everything.

He found Brandon in his corner office, his head burrowed over a stack of memos.

"Nick Garroway, reporting for duty," he said.

Brandon looked up, looking weary. "I've been here since six o'clock. Couldn't sleep."

"Me either."

"I called Cathy a little while ago," Brandon said. "Dad was demanding a cappuccino with three sugars, a cheese Danish and today's *Wall Street Journal*. She had the nurse bring him a clementine, a hard-boiled egg, a slice of whole-grain toast and bottled water, and gave him a gratitude journal to record his thoughts."

Nick smiled. "Thank heavens for Cathy."

"Right?" Brandon said with a nod.

"Well, I'm ready to start my day, my new role, at Garroway Paper," Nick said. "I'll buy a briefcase at lunch. No idea what you business types put in those, but I'm sure I'll find out fast."

Brandon stared at Nick for a moment, then stood and reached into his desk drawer. He pulled out a magnetic door placard and held it up. It read Nicholas Garroway.

"I can't remember the last time anyone called me Nicholas," Nick said, the sight of that thing making his stomach clench. He'd have to get over it. He was here now. He worked here. This was his future.

"Mom called you Nicholas," Brandon said.

Nick almost gasped. He hadn't expected Brandon to say that, let alone remember.

"She loved that name and liked using it," Brandon said. "You want to know what she said the night before she died?"

Nick felt his legs get wobbly and he sat down. So did Brandon.

He wasn't sure he did want to know.

Brandon was looking at the floor, then out the window. Finally he turned to face Nick. "She said, 'Nicholas always follows his heart. That's the way to happiness. The only way.'"

Now Nick did gasp. "She said that?"

Brandon's eyes filled with tears, and he nodded. "It was one of the last things she said. Other than 'I love you and your brother more than anything in the world. And your father, of course. The love of my life.' That was the last thing she said to me."

Tears stung Nick's eyes too. He hadn't been at the house that night; the tension between him and his brother and father was so high, and of course Nick hadn't expected to lose his mother that night. No one had. "But you said—"

"I was a stupid fourteen-year-old who hated you for being about to deploy. Stuff flew out of my mouth, anything I could think of to make you feel like the hell I felt."

Nick sucked in a breath. "I did already."

"I'm sorry," Brandon said, wiping at his eyes. "I'm so sorry. For being a terrible brother. And a terrible person. But when I thought I might lose dad, all I could think was, I have Nick back, I have Nick back, I have Nick back. And all those old feelings came back too, you know? I mean from before, when we were close."

Nick could barely find his voice. "We're close now."

Brandon took a breath. "I want to be the person Heather deserves. That her baby deserves. So this?" he said, holding up the placard. He stood and opened the window, then chucked the name sign right out of it. Right below the window was a gated area with bushes blocking the heating systems, so Nick had no doubt Nicholas Garroway was lying in those bushes somewhere.

His brother had just thrown his name sign out the window.

Nick stared at him. *"What?"*

"You *don't* belong here, Nick. I finally get it. You've been saying that your whole life, but I didn't want to hear it. I didn't care. I only saw you through my eyes, not as you were. Are. You were meant to be a soldier. Now you're meant to be a rancher. And you're meant to be with Brooke and the twins. You have to follow your heart, like Mom said you did. Do it now."

You're meant to be with Brooke and the twins. He'd put his feelings for the Timber family in a square box called Responsible For. They'd been on his checklist and he understood checklists. Why had he been able to walk away from Garroway Paper when it came to "responsibility" but not Brooke and her twins? He'd immediately become her nanny. He'd felt solely responsible for her and the twins' well-being. So why hadn't that sense of commitment extended to the family business? And if it was a sense of commitment, why couldn't he actually *commit* to Brooke? None of this made any sense.

He'd never been able to answer these questions, and they'd kept him up at night all week.

"One thing at a time," Nick said. "I'm on overload as it is."

"Go buy your ranch," his brother said. "I'll even help you name those chickens you want. And propose to Brooke already. Wedlock Creek Jewelers has really nice diamond rings."

He swallowed, keeping his gaze out the window instead of on his brother, who was eyeing him with the look of a guy who thought he knew the deal.

Nick *did* belong with Brooke and the Timber twins. That was never in doubt. From a taking-care-of-them standpoint. But could he be with her the way she wanted and needed? A husband, a father?

How could Brandon have this all figured out when Nick was so far behind?

Something occurred to him just then. Wouldn't marrying Brooke be the *ultimate* in taking responsibility for her and the babies? When he looked at it that way, he felt instantly more comfortable.

"Where's the jewelry shop?" Nick asked.

Brandon grinned. "Two doors down from Java Jane's. Next to the florist. Might as well pick up a bouquet too."

"Wait, did you propose to Heather?" Nick asked.

Brandon grinned. "Sure did. She said no. For now.

She told me to ask her again in a month. And a month after that."

"That sounds like a plan," Nick said. He had a feeling that, despite how short a time Heather had known his brother, she knew exactly how to deal with him. He wouldn't be surprised if Heather turned him down a month from now, but said yes when they were together three months. She'd probably insist on waiting a year to actually marry.

Marry. He mentally shook his head, but the word didn't dislodge as it usually did when he tried to relate it to himself. It stayed there, hanging out in his brain. Marry. Marriage. Husband and wife.

He could take care of Brooke and the twins. And have them with him all of the time. That was what he wanted. But something was missing, something he couldn't put his finger on.

Maybe he should stop thinking so much and just *do*, act.

And now that he didn't have to work this morning, that was his new plan.

Chapter Fourteen

On Monday night, at around six o'clock, Brooke couldn't take the suspense. She had to know how Nick's first day at Garroway Paper had gone.

She sat at the kitchen table, sipped her iced tea and pulled out her phone, dying to call him, but she opted for a text. She was about to hit Send when the doorbell rang.

Nick.

"I was sending you a text," she said.

His expression immediately changed. "Everything okay?" he asked, peering past her. "House is quiet. Twins are all right?"

"There's a whole area of existence beyond whether I'm okay or not," she said, feeling a frown edge her lips.

"I care about you, Brooke. You know that."

"I do know that," she said, holding back the sigh and opening the door wider for him to step in.

"So, what you were texting me about?" he asked as he followed her into the living room. He stopped to pet Snowball and Smudge, who were sitting on the back of the sofa.

"I was dying to hear how your first day at Garroway Paper went."

"My brother had a name placard made for me. He must have had it for years. And this morning, not ten minutes into my arrival, he opened his office window and tossed it out. Literally threw the thing out the window."

Brooke's mouth dropped open. "Really?"

Nick laughed. "Brandon is one complicated guy. Deeper than I realized. He's been doing some heavy thinking, and between Dad's health and falling madly in love, and all that's happened since I've been back in town, he's started to see things differently."

"Wow. I'm really glad to hear it."

"And I have too, Brooke."

She tilted her head. "What do you mean? You're not going to stay on with the company, are you?"

He shook his head. "No. But what I am going to do depends on your answer to a question."

Curiosity bloomed inside her. "What question?"

He got down on one knee, and she gasped. He pulled a velvet box out of his pocket and opened the top, revealing a beautiful diamond ring that twinkled at her. God, it was gorgeous. Square and surrounded by tiny diamonds on a gold band. "Will you marry me, Brooke?

Spending my life taking care of you and those babies I love as if they're my own will make me very happy."

Oh. Her heart sunk, and her stomach flopped—in a bad way. "I thought you said you also started to see things differently."

He stood up, staring at her, confusion in his eyes. "I have. That's why I'm here. Proposing. But you don't exactly look happy."

"Nick, it's a beautiful ring. And believe me, as a woman who's madly in love with you, I want to scream yes at the top of my lungs. But unless you can say you want to marry me because you're in love with me, and that's why you want to be my husband, my answer is no. I told you I'm not looking to be rescued. I'm looking to be *loved*."

"But—" He stopped speaking, as though realizing he had no argument.

Because either he loved her or he didn't.

"Brooke, I—"

"Do you love me, Nick?" she asked.

He stared at her. Unwavering. "I care so much about you and the twins. I want to be with you three. I want us to be a family."

"Me too," she said. "But you didn't answer my question. And we both know why not. So I think you should go."

Her eyes stung. She wanted him gone so she could run upstairs and fling herself on her bed and just cry it out.

She turned away, sending up a prayer that he'd say, "Of course I love you. I love you so much." But instead she heard the door close gently behind him as he left.

And then she did run upstairs and cry.

* * *

"Can't you sneak me in a chocolate milkshake? Something besides this god-awful green tea," Jeb asked Nick, grimacing at the steaming mug Cathy had brought in a few minutes ago. He'd been released from the hospital yesterday and was convalescing on his favorite recliner in his living room, with Fritz in his dog bed near Jeb's feet.

Nick laughed. "Sorry, I want you heart-healthy too."

Jeb patted Nick's hand. "I'm glad to hear that. I wasn't always fair to you—or there for you—but you stuck by me. What you said at the wedding, what you wrote in our wedding card, I'll tell you, you brought tears to my eyes."

"I love you, Dad. It's that simple."

I love you. It's that simple.

He sat up straight, the words echoing in his head, on his tongue.

I love you.

It was as though a Mack Truck had swerved into the living room and had run right over Nick, shaking loose something in his very thick skull.

He loved Brooke. It really was that simple.

His father was staring at him. "So, who's getting married first. You and Brooke, or Brandon and Heather?"

Nick laughed. "Anyone's guess."

"Ah, so it is true. I told Cathy I didn't think there was anything going on between you and the wedding planner, but Cathy told me she knew love when she saw it, and she said she saw it plain as day on your face. Isn't that something? A newcomer to the family knows you better than I do. I hope we can change that."

Nick gave his dad's hand a gentle squeeze. "We will, Dad."

"I have some big news," Jeb said. "I've told your brother on the phone, right before you arrived, since it affects him directly." Nick's curiosity was piqued. "Cathy and I have decided to get out of dodge. We're buying the Sagebrush Sanctuary and Retreat from her friend and moving there. We'll be doing a little re-structuring, as suits us, as we learn the business better. I'll be Chief Financial Officer, and Cathy will run the yoga and meditation program. Heather promises to find a replacement for herself and train him or her before she moves to Wedlock Creek."

Wow. "That all sounds great," Nick said, blown away. And not. It made perfect sense, actually. "How'd Brandon take it?"

"You know, I was surprised at how well he did take the news. He said he's come to some big realizations lately. And he knows he was born to take over Garroway Paper and run it now that I'm moving on. He also said that if the baby he and Heather are expecting grows up to be bored by paper, that'll be fine too. 'Everyone has to follow their heart,' he said."

Nick felt his own heart grow two sizes bigger. "Wonders never cease, do they?" he asked with a smile.

"No, and what a good thing that is," Jeb said. "Life is one big surprise. Sometimes in a good way, sometimes in a bad way, and sometimes in a bad way that delivers you where you need to be after all."

Nick nodded. That sure was right.

Jeb took a sip of his tea. "I'm slowly—key word being *slowly*—getting used to this stuff." He set down the mug and resettled under the blanket, on the recliner, with his eyes starting to drift closed, and Nick was almost glad to be able to sneak away a bit earlier than he'd intended.

He had a proposal to get right.

"Ga ba!" Mikey said, flinging his chew toy at Brooke for the thousandth time in his young life. His gummy grin was too irresistible, so Brooke gave him a raspberry on his onesie-clad tummy.

"Ba ba da?" Mikey said, tilting his head.

Brooke stared at the adorable baby, marveling that it sounded as though he were asking something. Huh.

I know what you're asking. You want to know where Nick is. You miss him. Like I do.

I could have been wearing that ring. I could be planning my own wedding. My dream wedding. Not that it would be her dream wedding if it wasn't her dream situation. *Still, I could have settled for what I could have instead of what I really want.*

Her grandmother would turn over. *Don't settle when it's less than you deserve, or then "just okay" will become the new normal,* Aggie Timber had said more than once. *And "just okay" is not all that okay.*

The doorbell rang, and Brooke had a feeling it was nosy Amy from across the street, who'd darted over a couple of hours ago, while walking her dog, to mention that she hadn't seen "that handsome manny" in a while and ask if he still worked for Brooke.

Brooke had said something about hearing one of

the twins and had dashed inside. God, what she would give to move away from these nosy gossips. She could move to the country and build a farmhouse-wedding chic office, maybe a yurt like at the Sagebrush Sanctuary and Retreat.

She smiled at the thought. Maybe she should think about buying a bigger house out of town, where you got much more for your money, a place where her twins could have some real land to play on and she could adopt the dog she'd always wanted, not that Smudge and Snowball might approve. She'd stay within fifteen minutes of town and her farmhouse-chic she-shed office would appeal to a range of clients. The Satlers would love it. She had no doubt.

This is what it's about, boys, she thought, her gaze on her sons. No time for a broken heart. No time for crushed hopes and dreams. Onward and upward, forward thoughts. The future.

But then she pictured Nick in his white linen shirt, with his blue eyes all intense on her, and she missed him so much, her legs wobbled. She sank down on a chair, feeling her heart aching.

Who was she kidding? Her heart was killing her. It would be a long while before she'd get over Nick Garroway.

The doorbell rang again. Oh blast. *That woman does not give up.* She wiped away her tears and stalked to the door, prepared to tell Amy that yes, her nanny had moved on, and to give her a piece of her mind about minding her own beeswax.

But it was Nick. Standing there in her doorway, looking so gorgeous, she could barely breathe.

"You asked me a question yesterday and I didn't answer," Nick said. "You know why?"

Oh God. She really didn't think she could handle this a second time. The first was bad enough. "I know why."

He shook his head. "Nope. You thought you did. But the reason was that, sort of like my dad, I had some kind of blockage right here," he said, putting his hand over his heart. "You cleared it up so fast, I couldn't handle it. Know why?"

She bit her lip, not quite sure where he was going with this. "Why?"

"Because I *do* love you. So much, Brooke. I want to marry you because I'm deeply, hopelessly, completely in love with you. And those little imps listening behind you in their swings have known it the whole time. From day one."

She laughed. "I agree. They always knew."

"Yeah, they did. All that 'ba ga, da ba' stuff. Code for 'he loves her. He's going to be our daddy one day.'"

She flung her arms around him and he picked her up off the ground and held her. "I love you too. So much." She kissed him, never wanting this moment to end.

"If we get married at the Wedlock Creek Chapel, will we have another set of twins?" he asked, setting her down, but keeping his arms around her.

"Maybe triplets," she said with a grin. "Or quadruplets. Want to risk it?"

His eyes widened. "You made me believe in magic, so honestly? No. I'm good with two right now. Maybe a couple years from now, we'll renew our vows there and really see what happens."

Brooke's heart had runneth over to the point that

she could barely form words. She took a deep breath to get some air in her lungs. "I like it. You know what wedding I'd like to plan for myself? An elopement. To somewhere crazy-fun, like Las Vegas."

"So, no planning," he said.

"Right. Just you and me and a quickie-wedding chapel."

"And the wedding night. Can't forget that."

"You know what else I was thinking? About moving to the country. Having a farmhouse-chic she-shed of an office that will make my clients drool when they drive out for meetings. Kind of fits with your whole plan to buy a ranch."

"I was going to give up the ranch idea to move in here, but I've found the perfect place, and it's still available. It's called the Three Dog Ranch, so we'll have to adopt three dogs to live there. House rules. Think these two can deal?" he asked, nodding at the cats.

Smudge and Snowball wrapped around his legs, rubbing their faces against his calves.

"They've always wanted to be indoor cats *and* barn cats," she said. She bit her lip. "You know what? I feel like my grandmother is looking down at me and smiling."

"I feel that way about my mom now too," he said, wrapping her in another hug. "Turns out her motto was Follow Your Heart. It's a good one."

"I agree. Always follow your heart."

"Ga ba!" Morgan shouted.

"Ba ga da!" Mikey added.

Nick pulled her close and kissed her. "Think those Timber twins would like to become the Garroway twins?"

Tears poked at her eyes. "I think they'd love that."

"I promise to be a father worthy of them," he said.

She touched his cheek, loving him so much, she was surprised she didn't burst into a million pieces. "That's a good new promise."

He held her close and leaned his head on top of hers. "I can't wait to start forever with you and our boys."

"Me too," she whispered. With their boys and her manny-for-life.

* * * * *

Check out Melissa Senate's next book,
Rust Creek Falls Cinderella
the second book in the Montana Mavericks:
Six Brides for Six Brothers continuity,
coming in August 2019 from
Harlequin Special Edition!

And catch up with the rest of
the Wyoming Multiples stories:

The Baby Switch
Detective Barelli's Legendary Triplets
Wyoming Christmas Surprise
To Keep Her Baby

Available now!

Get 4 FREE REWARDS!

We'll send you 2 FREE Books plus 2 FREE Mystery Gifts.

Harlequin® Special Edition books feature heroines finding the balance between their work life and personal life on the way to finding true love.

FREE
Value Over
$20

YES! Please send me 2 FREE Harlequin® Special Edition novels and my 2 FREE gifts (gifts are worth about $10 retail). After receiving them, if I don't wish to receive any more books, I can return the shipping statement marked "cancel." If I don't cancel, I will receive 6 brand-new novels every month and be billed just $4.99 per book in the U.S. or $5.74 per book in Canada. That's a savings of at least 12% off the cover price! It's quite a bargain! Shipping and handling is just 50¢ per book in the U.S. and 75¢ per book in Canada.* I understand that accepting the 2 free books and gifts places me under no obligation to buy anything. I can always return a shipment and cancel at any time. The free books and gifts are mine to keep no matter what I decide.

235/335 HDN GMY2

Name (please print)

Address   Apt. #

City   State/Province   Zip/Postal Code

Mail to the Reader Service:
IN U.S.A. P.O. Box 1341, Buffalo, NY 14240-8531
IN CANADA: P.O. Box 603, Fort Erie, Ontario L2A 5X3

Want to try 2 free books from another series! Call 1-800-873-8635 or visit www.ReaderService.com.

---

*Terms and prices subject to change without notice. Prices do not include sales taxes, which will be charged (if applicable) based on your state or country of residence. Canadian residents will be charged applicable taxes. Offer not valid in Quebec. This offer is limited to one order per household. Books received may not be as shown. Not valid for current subscribers to Harlequin® Special Edition books. All orders subject to approval. Credit or debit balances in a customer's account(s) may be offset by any other outstanding balance owed by or to the customer. Please allow 4 to 6 weeks for delivery. Offer available while quantities last.

Your Privacy—The Reader Service is committed to protecting your privacy. Our Privacy Policy is available online at www.ReaderService.com or upon request from the Reader Service. We make a portion of our mailing list available to reputable third parties that offer products we believe may interest you. If you prefer that we not exchange your name with third parties, or if you wish to clarify or modify your communication preferences, please visit us at www.ReaderService.com/consumerschoice or write to us at Reader Service Preference Service, P.O. Box 9062, Buffalo, NY 14240-9062. Include your complete name and address.

HSE19R2

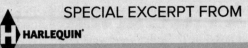
*To give the orphaned triplets they're guardians of the
stability they need, Lulu McCabe and Sam Kirkland
decide to jointly adopt them. But when it's discovered
their marriage wasn't actually annulled, they have
to prove to the courts they're responsible—
by renewing their vows!*

Read on for a sneak preview of Cathy Gillen Thacker's
Their Inherited Triplets,
the next book in the
Texas Legends: The McCabes miniseries.

"The two of you are still married," Liz said.

"Still?" Lulu croaked.

Sam asked, "What are you talking about?"

"More to the point, how do you know this?" Lulu
demanded, the news continuing to hit her like a gut punch.

Travis looked down at the papers in front of him.
"Official state records show you eloped in the Double
Knot Wedding Chapel in Memphis, Tennessee, on
Monday, March 14, nearly ten years ago. Alongside
another couple, Peter and Theresa Thompson, in a double
wedding ceremony."

Lulu gulped. "But our union was never legal," she
pointed out, trying to stay calm, while Sam sat beside her
in stoic silence.

Liz countered, "Ah, actually, it is legal. In fact, it's still
valid to this day."

Sam reached over and took her hand in his, much as he had the first time they had been in this room together. "How is that possible?" Lulu asked weakly.

"We never mailed in the certificate of marriage, along with the license, to the state of Tennessee," Sam said.

"And for our union to be recorded and therefore legal, we had to have done that," Lulu reiterated.

"Well, apparently, the owners of the Double Knot Wedding Chapel did, and your marriage was recorded. And is still valid to this day, near as we can tell. Unless you two got a divorce or an annulment somewhere else? Say another country?" Travis prodded.

"Why would we do that? We didn't know we were married," Sam returned.

Don't miss
Their Inherited Triplets *by Cathy Gillen Thacker,*
available August 2019 wherever
Harlequin® *Special Edition books and ebooks are sold.*

www.Harlequin.com

Looking for more satisfying love stories
with community and family at their core?

Check out **Harlequin® Special Edition**
and **Love Inspired®** books!

New books available every month!

CONNECT WITH US AT:

Facebook.com/groups/HarlequinConnection

Facebook.com/HarlequinBooks

Twitter.com/HarlequinBooks

Instagram.com/HarlequinBooks

Pinterest.com/HarlequinBooks

ReaderService.com

**ROMANCE WHEN
YOU NEED IT**

HFGENRE2018

*Read on for a sneak peek at
the first funny and heart-tugging book in Jo McNally's
Rendezvous Falls series,* Slow Dancing at Sunrise!

"I'd have thought the idea of me getting caught in a rainstorm would make your day."

He gave her a quick glance. Just because she was off-limits didn't mean he was blind.

"Trust me, it did." Luke slowed the truck and reached behind the seat to grab his zippered hoodie hanging there. Whitney looked down and her cheeks flamed when she realized how her clothes were clinging to her. She snatched the hoodie from his hand before he could give it to her, and thrust her arms into it without offering any thanks. Even the zipper sounded pissed off when she yanked it closed.

"Perfect. Another guy with more testosterone than manners. Nice to know it's not just a Chicago thing. Jackasses are everywhere."

Luke frowned. He'd been having fun at her expense, figuring she'd give it right back to him as she had before. But her words hinted at a story that didn't reflect well on men in general. She'd been hurt. He shouldn't care. But that quick dimming of the fight in her eyes made him feel ashamed. *That* was a new experience.

A flash of lightning made her flinch. But the thunder didn't follow as quickly as the last time. The storm was moving off. He drove from the vineyard into the parking lot and over to the main house. The sound of the rain on the roof was less angry. But Whitney wasn't. She was clutching his sweatshirt around herself, her knuckles white. From anger? Embarrassment? Both? Luke shook his head.

"Look, I thought I was doing the right thing, driving up there." He rubbed the back of his neck and grimaced, remembering how sweaty and filthy he still was. "It's not my fault you walked out of the woods soaking wet. I mean, I try not to be a jackass, but I'm still a man. And I *did* offer my hoodie."

Whitney's chin pointed up toward the second floor of the main house. Her neck was long and graceful. There was a vein pulsing at the base of it. She blinked a few times, and for a horrifying moment, he thought there might be tears shimmering there in her eyes. *Damn it.* The last thing he needed was to have Helen's niece *crying* in his truck. He opened his mouth to say something—anything—but she beat him to it.

"I'll concede I wasn't prepared for rain." Her mouth barely moved, her words forced through clenched teeth. "But a gentleman would have looked away or…something."

His low laughter was enough to crack that brittle shell of hers. She turned to face him, eyes wide.

"See, Whitney, that's where you made your biggest mistake." He shrugged. "It wasn't going out for a day hike with a storm coming." He talked over her attempted objection. "Your *biggest* mistake was thinking I'm any kind of gentleman."

The corner of her mouth tipped up into an almost smile. "But you said you weren't a jackass."

"There's a hell of a lot of real estate between jackass and gentleman, babe."

Her half smile faltered, then returned. That familiar spark appeared in her eyes. The crack in her veneer had been repaired, and the sharp edge returned to her voice. Any other guy might have been annoyed, but Luke was oddly relieved to see Whitney back in fighting form.

"The fact that you just referred to me as 'babe' tells me you're a lot closer to jackass than you think."

He lifted his shoulder. "I never told you which end of the spectrum I fell on."

The rain had slowed to a steady drizzle. She reached for the door handle, looking over her shoulder with a smirk.

"Actually, I'm pretty sure you just did."

She hurried up the steps to the covered porch. He waited, but she didn't look back before going into the house. Her energy still filled the cab of the truck, and so did her scent. Spicy, woodsy, rain soaked. Finally coming to his senses, he threw the truck into Reverse and headed back toward the carriage house. He needed a long shower. A long *cold* one.

Don't miss
Jo McNally's Slow Dancing at Sunrise,
available July 2019 from HQN Books!

www.Harlequin.com

Love Harlequin romance?

DISCOVER.

Be the first to find out about promotions,
news and exclusive content!

Facebook.com/HarlequinBooks

Twitter.com/HarlequinBooks

Instagram.com/HarlequinBooks

Pinterest.com/HarlequinBooks

ReaderService.com

EXPLORE.

Sign up for the Harlequin e-newsletter and
download a free book from any series at
TryHarlequin.com.

CONNECT.

Join our Harlequin community to share
your thoughts and connect with other
romance readers!
Facebook.com/groups/HarlequinConnection

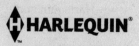

HARLEQUIN®

**ROMANCE WHEN
YOU NEED IT**